"Do you believe in love at first sight, Laurian?"

"I didn't."

"Do you now . . . ? I loved you the moment I saw you," he said thoughtfully. "I'd never seen anybody so vitally alive and shining as you when you put down that bowl of flowers and turned to meet us last Saturday."

"Was it only eight days ago? It's not possible. I've known you always."

"I knew in that first moment that we belonged . . . didn't you?" he questioned.

"Yes."

"Why do we talk?" he asked roughly, and took her in his arms.

Also Available in Beagle Books Editions:

Wonderful Down-to-Earth Stories
of Life and Love by

IRIS BROMIGE

The Brightest Bestselling Romance Novelist

Laurian Vale
Iris Bromige

#33

BALLANTINE BOOKS • NEW YORK

First published 1952 by Hodder & Stoughton Ltd.

SBN 345-26689-7-095

This edition published by arrangement with
Hodder & Stoughton Ltd.

First Printing: February, 1975

Printed in the United States of America

A Beagle Book

BALLANTINE BOOKS
A Division of Random House, Inc.
201 East 50th Street, New York, N.Y. 10022

Chapter One

JOHN VALE LOWERED his paper and watched his daughter cross the lawn with Philip Dallas. She walked well, he thought: a free swinging action and a straight back. None of this mincing along in high heels or flapping about in shoes without toes or heels, and most young females these days seemed to belong to one or other of these schools, both of which he abominated. As they emerged from the shade of the beech tree, the sunshine lit up the coppery tones in Laurian's brown hair and reminded him that his wife's hair had once been auburn. They made a good-looking couple, Laurian and young Dallas. A very satisfactory match in every way. He hoped Philip would come to the point quickly and stand no nonsense.

He settled in his deck-chair as the couple passed through the wicket gate at the end of the garden and disappeared into the meadow beyond, and picked up his paper again, but he couldn't concentrate. He had watched with inward amusement Philip's moves to get Laurian away for a walk in spite of her determination to write some report or other for the Larksmere Social Club. The fact that he had succeeded added further support to the growing conviction that Philip's quiet, easy manner concealed a strength of mind and purpose above the average, and strong-mindedness was the quality which John Vale respected above all. He looked across at his wife, who was doing some embroidery with the detached air which used to infuriate him but to which he had grown accustomed.

"Think Laurian will accept Dallas?"

1

Helen Vale looked up slowly, as though returning reluctantly from a far distant land which only she inhabited.

"Marry Philip?"

"Yes. What else? It's obvious enough that he wants her to."

"I don't think she's in love with him. She has plenty of time."

"It would be a good match. Philip's the right type for Laurian."

"In what way?"

"In every way," replied her husband curtly. "Character, position and breeding. Don't want to see Laurian get tied up to any Tom, Dick or Harry. She's our only child. Good family, Philip's."

"A pity he is the younger son, if you're thinking of the title."

"I am not."

"Aren't you?"

His lips tightened for a moment at his wife's gentle irony. Then he said with deliberation:

"I am not, though I don't think a baronet for a father-in-law will prove any handicap to Laurian. I'm a self-made man, and proud of it, and I've no time for snobs. But if I've got the brass, Philip's side can provide the culture. It's a good team-up. Have you any objections?"

"None at all. I like Philip Dallas. But Laurian, being your daughter, will decide for herself, and our approval or otherwise won't influence her, I fancy."

"H'm. Has she got anybody else in mind?"

"Not as far as I know. She seems to like to ring the changes on her escorts. She has several."

"No doubt. Money has a good smell, particularly when it's lined up with a girl as easy to look at as Laurian. That's why I'd like to see her settled with Philip. She's charged up with vitality, and has nothing important to spill it on. That's dangerous. An early marriage with a sound man and a family to absorb her will be the best thing in the world for her."

His wife continued with her embroidery, a faint smile hovering round her thin lips. Her husband had hammered out his design on life with a ruthlessness which had been crowned with success. In only one respect had the design deviated from his conception: she had failed to bear him the sons he had craved. But if he tried to include Laurian's life in his design, he would probably learn for the second time that he was not omnipotent, and he would learn it from the person who was dearest to him.

Silence fell between them until he threw his paper aside and stood up.

"When Sutton and Brenver arrive, send them up to the study. I've a report to go through."

"Brenver?"

"Yes. A young engineer of ours. He's bringing blueprints of the proposed installation at the new factory. If that fool of a doctor says I can't get to work, work must get to me."

"What did Dr. Garson say this morning?"

"Usual bright formula. Doing fine. Give it another week."

"Are you going to?"

"No. I shall be back on the job on Wednesday. We've a Board meeting on Thursday and I can't spare any more time doodling here. Garson's an old woman. All this fuss over an appendix!"

His wife, knowing better than to argue, watched him walk back to the house. In any case, she thought, he would be better at work than fuming at enforced idleness at home. His work was his life.

She dropped her embroidery in her lap and leaned back in the chair, relaxed, glad to be alone with the garden. In May, it was at its freshest and, perhaps, loveliest. It was true that the roses were only just in bud, but the hawthorn hedge was white with blossom, its petals scattered over the grass below like confetti, and the laburnum tree beside her was a shower of gold. A bed of lilies of the valley against the wall filled the air with their fragrance: lovely, delicate little flowers with their smooth, furled leaves, they were among her dearest treasures. The lupin spikes in the border were turning colour, and there were masses of columbines and pyrethrums in flower. May-time, when everything was fresh and bright, before the passage of summer ripened and dimmed; when all was promise and nothing jaded. Laurian's time. And as she watched the shadowy pattern cast by the birch tree on the red brick wall of the house, finding it infinitely pleasing, she felt a little sorry for Philip.

Laurian twisted the cowslip in her fingers as she listened, then carefully tucked it through a buttonhole of her frock before she answered.

"I'm sorry, Philip, but I'm afraid the answer is no. I like you very much, but only as a friend."

"I see. I was afraid of that. Tell me one thing, Laurian. Is there anybody else?"

"No. I'm heart-free, and I want to stay that way for quite a time yet."

"Marriage doesn't appeal to you?"

"Not yet. I'm not ready to settle down. I enjoy life as a free lance."

"Enjoyment of life doesn't necessarily cease when you get married, you know."

She smiled up at him.

"Perhaps not. But I want to keep my freedom a little longer."

"Which all boils down to the fact that you don't love me. Well, I can wait."

"It's no good, Philip. I do know my own mind. You'll only be wasting your time."

"Whether I win or lose, time spent on you will never be wasted. I love you too much for that. And I don't give up easily when so much is at stake. You are, at least, happy to be friends?"

She laid a hand on his arm impulsively.

"Of course, Philip. Always."

"Good. That's a basis I can hope to build on."

"Now be a dear and let me get back to my report. I must get it off this evening."

He swung her off the stile and held her for a moment, studying her gravely. Then he gave her an odd little smile.

"What a tantalising young thing you are, to be sure!"

"In what way?"

"Never mind. How many young men have kissed that inviting mouth of yours, I wonder?"

"Are you thinking of adding to the number?"

"Not just now. I'm after the serious stuff. Past the age for youthful frolics. If I can't have the whole cake, I don't want to nibble at the icing with the young bloods."

They began to walk back across the meadow, and Laurian stole a glance at the tall, thin figure of her companion. She had accepted Philip Dallas's attentions with the same easy lightheartedness which she accorded to all her friends, and she had many, but it occurred to her now that she really knew less of Philip than of any of them. He had always stood apart from the others, for at thirty-one he was several years older than most, and he took no part in the activities of the Larksmere Social Club, of which Laurian was a leading light, and from which her friends were mainly drawn. She knew that he was Sir Robert Dallas's younger son, that he and his brother Julian were directors of the publishing house which the family had founded over a hundred years ago, that Sir Robert, whose health was failing, lived in the South of France, and that an aunt kept Bryony House going for his two sons.

These facts she knew, but what did she know of the person Philip Dallas? Her eyes told her that he was tall and thin, with black hair and dark grey eyes, a pale, clean-shaven face and features which individually were unremarkable, but collectively seemed to carry a quiet distinction. That seemed to be the keynote of Philip's personality as she knew it: quietness. A calm, unhurried manner, a quiet voice, and, she was sure, a quiet mind. It was a quality which was not without attraction for her since it was so rare in her home life where her father's ebullience and her own kept it at bay. And beneath the quietness? She knew very little. A sensitive intelligence, a personal reserve, a certain fastidiousness; there was not much else she could fasten on.

"Do you find life good, on the whole, Philip?" she asked suddenly, in an effort to penetrate further.

"That's a large question to have shot at one out of the blue. Yes, I think, having come to terms with it, I do find it pretty fair. I'd say it's largely what you make of it."

"What do you mean by coming to terms with it?"

"Oh, by accepting it as it is, not kicking against the unpleasant bits, not expecting too much of human nature."

"That sounds a bit dim."

"It isn't really. But then, by temperament you're a fighter and I'm a strategist. Does your life satisfy you?"

"Yes. Up to a point. I enjoy it. Have a good time and all that. But I get very restless sometimes. Feel I want something to bite on. Penny says it's because I've been spoiled and have always had everything I wanted. She says the salt's lacking."

"That's a point, certainly. Your local activities keep you pretty well occupied, I gather?"

"Oh, I do a good deal of work for the local W.V.S. and take dancing classes twice a week for the Women's Institute and the Social Club, and I'm secretary of the Club, as you know. That keeps me busy, but it doesn't seem to add up to much and sometimes I feel stifled."

"H'm. Larksmere is a bit limited, I agree. Did I hear your father grumbling about some wild-cat scheme of yours when I arrived on the scene today?"

"You did. I want to open a dancing school in Kingsford, but Dad needs a little persuading about it. I always wanted to be a dancer, you know, but Dad would never hear of it. Anyway, I wasn't good enough to get far, I guess, and I compromised by taking various exams, hoping I might teach. Then Mother had a long illness, and afterwards we went to Switzerland for six months, so I was really side-tracked, and I've just let local affairs occupy me since then. I suppose if anything is sufficiently important to you, though, you don't get side-tracked."

"No."

She realised, as he opened the gate for her, that she had intended to find out more about her companion, instead of which she had enlarged upon herself.

"I'll just collect my parcel and say good-bye," said Philip.

"Won't you stay to tea?"

"Thank you, no. I've a very bulky manuscript to get through this weekend."

The garden was deserted and they went into the house. Mrs. Vale met them in the hall.

"Hullo. You're not going, Philip, are you?"

"Afraid I must, Mrs. Vale. Will you say good-bye to your husband for me?"

"Of course. He's in conference with his secretary and an engineer from the factory. You look tired, Philip. I believe you work too hard."

Philip smiled as he picked up his black felt hat. He had called in on his way home from London and his dark town clothes looked particularly sombre beside Laurian's green linen dress and white shoes.

"Everyone likes to be told that they work too hard, Mrs. Vale, but I don't really earn that medal."

Laurian and her mother stood in the porch and waved as he drove off.

"Philip's an odd person. You never really know what he's thinking," observed Laurian.

"You might if he thought you wanted to."

Laurian hesitated, then said a shade defiantly:

"Well, when I refused to marry him this afternoon, I really couldn't tell whether it was a terrible disappointment or just a slight setback to his plans."

"I could," replied Mrs. Vale quietly.

"You're a very seeing woman, like most people who don't talk much," said Laurian lightly. Then she frowned at her reflection in the hall mirror. "You know, I hate hurting people, Mummy, but it wasn't any use."

"Then you were quite right, dear. I think you're too young to marry yet, anyway. You're only a child."

"Twenty-three last week, you know."

"It's not possible. Run and pick some fresh flowers for the sitting-room, dear. They're a little faded. I must tell Penny we've two extra for tea."

"One being the pilot fish, I gather."

"I don't know why you dislike Mr. Sutton so much. He's invaluable to your father."

"I don't dislike him. Pilot fish are useful little things to their masters. Who is the other visitor?"

"A Mr. Brenver. He's an engineer from the factory. The polyanthas will look nicest for that flat bowl, dear."

> "I go, I go; look how I go—
> Swifter than arrow from the Tartar's bow,"

quoted Laurian, dancing down the hall into the sitting room to remove the offending flowers.

She appeared a moment later with the bowl balanced on her head and swayed down the hall towards the garden with undulating hips. Mrs. Vale smiled and shook her head. John was going to be angry, but their daughter's gay vitality would never submit to chains.

As Laurian was putting the bowl of fresh flowers on the table, her father walked in with his two associates in tow.

"Ah, there you are, Laurian my dear. Was that Philip's car I heard drive off?"

The old fox, thought Laurian, smiling at him; he never missed anything.

"Yes, Dad. He couldn't stay. Good afternoon, Mr. Sutton."

"Good afternoon, Miss Vale."

"And now, my dear, let me introduce Mr. Brenver. Brenver, my daughter."

Her eyes rested on the newcomer with interest. He

was pleasant to look at: average height, slight build, with fair hair and lively blue eyes. As his hand grasped hers, he looked straight at her and she sensed the quickening of his interest with her own. They seemed to make contact immediately.

Laurian chatted away gaily as she passed teacups and sandwiches, teasing Howard Sutton a little, turning a guileless face to her father, who was, she knew, wondering why Philip had gone, and stealing a glance now and again at Brenver. Her father prevented any lingering after tea by more or less dismissing the two men. Sutton had driven Brenver down in the prim little car which in Laurian's opinion was so well suited to her father's private secretary. She watched him now, as, brief-case in hand, he stood in the porch listening to her father's final instructions. He was the most negative person she had ever seen, and yet she knew he was shrewd enough and that her father, no mean judge, thought highly of him. If she shut her eyes, she would carry no definite impression of his face in her mind although she had seen him dozens of times. A pale young man: pale eyes, pale complexion, pale hair. A wraith. At heart, she despised him for his subservience.

Brenver was stowing some rolls of blueprints in the back of the car, and when he dropped one Laurian ran out and picked it up for him.

"Thanks so much." He lowered his voice. "Can I see you again?"

"Yes," she said breathlessly. "Telephone me here to-morrow morning at ten. I'll answer it."

He dived into the back of the car again as Sutton came up, and Laurian said good-bye and went in. She ran quickly up to her room, her cheeks flushed, her eyes shining, and decided that she must be a little mad. No man had ever affected her in this odd, exciting way before. She considered herself a level-headed person in such matters. She stood by the window and watched the car drive off, then sat down on the window-seat to collect herself and live over again the past hour.

While his daughter sat dreaming in her room, John Vale made his displeasure clear to his wife.

"But did Philip just accept it meekly?"

"I don't think he had any alternative, but Laurian gave me no details."

"She's a foolish child. Philip's a splendid match for her in every way. I've set my heart on it."

"But it's her heart that matters, John, and Philip hasn't touched it. She may come round to him in time, but she's very young. There's no hurry."

"You weren't as old as Laurian when you married me. I believe in early marriages. Better to have your children when you're young. Besides, married life will be good for Laurian. Make her settle down."

"But that's just it. She's not ready to settle down. Let her enjoy her youth, John. Don't try to push her into marriage. She means so much to you. I'm surprised that you want to lose her, since you'll miss her, I think, more than anybody."

"It's because she means so much to me that I want to see her marry the right man. She's a fine girl. She deserves the best, and, except for Philip, I've never seen a young man yet who matches up to her little finger. Look at the spineless specimens she brings here! Nincompoops, all of 'em."

"They're all young, John. You can't expect maturity on young shoulders."

"Too soft. Life's made too easy for 'em. At their age I was working twelve hours a day to support my mother and young brother and sister. Now, it seems to me, the young people would expect their mother to go out to work for them. They're soft through being spoiled—all of 'em."

"You've given your daughter the best of everything, made life soft for her. Why blame others for doing the same as you have done?"

"A girl's different. I don't expect womenfolk to go through the mill."

His wife raised her eyebrows delicately as she murmured:

"It depends what you mean by going through the mill."

"You're being perverse, Helen. You know what I mean. I think women should be protected as far as it lies in a man's power to do so. I don't like tough women any more than soft men. It's an out-of-date attitude, I grant you, but I hope I don't live to see the day when a woman's sphere is no longer in the home, and a man no longer shoulders his responsibilities. I may have spoiled Laurian, but any son of mine would have started at the bottom, the hard way, and earned his passage, I can tell you. If Laurian produces some grandsons for me, I hope they'll be brought up in the same way. They will if I have any say in it."

"You badly want grandchildren, don't you, John?"

"Yes, my dear. I'd like to see some boys in the family to inherit the business. I'm getting on, you know. Could do with some young blood in the offing."

"There are Miriam's boys."

"Val's useful, I admit. Doing quite well in the accounts department, I'm told. But not much drive. Young Tom's hopeless, of course. I wouldn't have him in the firm as a gift."

"I don't think he'd accept a job if you offered it. He wants to do something with his music. For a sixteen-year-old, he's quite promising."

"No, my dear. My nephews are not going to make much of a stir. Mediocre. But then, what can you expect from Miriam? Laurian's got my blood in her. I'll back her to produce some children with guts. I hope she'll change her mind about Philip. He's quiet, but the backbone's there. Think it would do any good if I had a talk with her?"

"The worst thing out."

But in spite of this discouragement from his wife, he did bring the subject up with Laurian that night after their game of chess. He made up his mind as he was putting the chessmen away.

"You always beat me, Dad. Don't know why I let myself get persuaded into it."

"Because you like a battle of wits and because you think that one day you'll catch me out."

"Maybe I will."

"So you sent Philip packing to-day?"

"Yes, darling," said Laurian lightly.

"I'm sorry."

"Are you? Don't you like me about the place?"

"Your happiness is more important to me than anything else in the world. You know that."

"But I am happy."

"There's nothing more important for a woman than to choose the right partner."

"But I'm the only one who can judge that."

"Are you? I wonder. I suppose you're waiting until you fall in love?"

"Of course."

"The worst possible state in which to make a sane judgment. All that goes. It's the wearing qualities that count."

Laurian wrinkled up her nose at him and smiled.

"I can't approach it as though I'm buying a winter coat, Dad."

"If more people did just that, my dear, there'd be fewer unhappy marriages."

"Well, I consider Philip's material is too dull," said his daughter, her brown eyes laughing at him. "Very hard wearing and in good taste, no doubt, but I think I'll wait for a model that's a little more dashing." She came round to his chair and kissed his forehead. "I'll go and fetch your nightcap, Dad, to stop your worrying. Do you know you're getting very thin on top?"

"I do. And don't let Penny add the whisky to my milk. She mistakes a teaspoon for a tablespoon."

"I'll put it in myself."

Her father smiled a little wrily, admitting defeat, as the door closed behind her. The room seemed dimmer for her going. She was an engaging young baggage. Always had been. Thought she could twist him round her little finger. Well, so she could, up to a point. Pity about Philip Dallas, though. Perhaps she'd change her

mind later. A good family the Dallases. Add their
breeding to the Vale money and Vale punch, and the
results should be pretty good. People didn't pay enough
attention to eugenics. And Laurian, his only child, was
such attractive bait for a fortune hunter. Still, for all
her gaiety, she had her head screwed on all right. She
had plenty of common sense. With affairs of the heart
though, common sense was apt to be overwhelmed. But
he was probably worrying for nothing. He'd try to give
Philip the tip to keep at it. But Philip wasn't exactly
the type of person to invite advice on his private affairs. Better leave it alone. He was a bit of a bull for
that sort of affair. Delicacy was not in his make-up and
he knew it. Blunt and straight from the shoulder—that
was John Vale. Always had been. Always would be.
And, he thought as he put the chessboard away in the
bookcase cupboard, nothing to be ashamed of in that.

Chapter Two

LAURIAN STOOD ON the bridge in St. James's Park and
watched the ducks. It was five minutes to six, and the
evening was warm and sunny. Rather a silly place to
arrange to meet, she thought. It might have been pouring with rain. But it was the first place she had thought
of when Brenver's voice at the other end of the wire
had asked her to name a rendezvous, and now fortune
had favoured them with a fine evening, so all was well.

Even now she could hardly believe that she, Laurian
Vale, had come up to London to meet a man who had
only appeared in her life three days ago and with
whom she had exchanged no more than a few sen-
tences. For a brief uncertain moment she felt that it
was crazy, that she shouldn't have come, and then she
saw him striding quickly along the path, and the uncertainty vanished, leaving a breathless sense of happiness
as though she were on a mountain peak with the loveliness of the world spread all about her.

"Hullo! I'm not late, am I?" he asked, as he took her hand.

"Dead on time. I hope this wasn't an awfully inconvenient place to choose."

"No, it's fine. Do you know, I was terrified that you wouldn't be here."

"Were you? Why?"

"Oh, second thoughts."

"I always keep my bargains. What shall we do?"

"I've booked a table at Scott's for dinner at eight. Until then, shall we just walk and talk?"

"I can't think of anything nicer. Come and look at the tulips for a start, Mr. . . . Brenver."

"Roy. All right?"

She laughed up at him.

"Quite all right."

He took her arm and steered her off the bridge.

"Do you think I've got an awful nerve?" he asked, his eyebrows raised as he quizzed her.

"I shouldn't be here if I did. I guess it was mutual."

"An honest girl with no coyness. You know, you *are* a find. I still can't believe that J. B. could have fathered such a gem. Tell me about yourself. What you do. What you like."

She told him, aware all the time of the pressure of his arm, of the vitality which matched her own and invited the full response of every part of her, mental and physical.

"Now what about you, Roy? I've talked enough. All I know of you is that you're an engineer in my father's firm. By the way, do you work at the office or the factory? I don't even know that."

"Fifty-fifty. I really act as liaison man between the factory manager and the office."

"Do you like it?"

"M'm. Pretty fair."

"Go on. Tell me more. Where do you live?"

"Highgate. I'm twenty-seven, ex-R.A.F., and I have no major vices. My health is good, my spirits excellent at the moment, and I am a bachelor. I have a weakness for girls with brown hair, dark brown eyes and a wide smile. Where are these tulips you were talking about?"

"I'd forgotten them. They're on the other side of the park now."

"Do they matter?"

She shook her head and they sat down on a seat beneath an elm tree. There they talked, exploring each other's minds eagerly, happily, so that time went by like a bird on the wing, and in the end they had to hurry to reach Scott's at the appointed hour.

As they sat down at their table and the waiter handed Roy the wine list. Laurian wondered whether he could really afford this. He was quite well dressed, but she guessed that his salary was modest, and she would have been quite happy with a salad and coffee at the Corner House if it suited his purse better. She was both too well mannered and too happy, however, to do anything but radiate delight at whatever he produced for her pleasure.

The waiter's usually impassive face relaxed indulgently as he served them. His expression of kindly irony seemed to say that it happened to most people once, and though it was all moonshine, it was pleasant to see.

"I wish the evening could go on for ever, but I must catch the nine-fifty from Victoria, Roy," Laurian said, as their coffee arrived.

"Whatever my lady commands. Do you have a long walk from Larksmere Station?"

"Twenty minutes if I walked. But I left the car at the station this morning. It's been a lovely evening."

"Yes." He looked across at her. "Now that I've found you, I'm not going to let you go. Not, that is, unless you shut yourself up in the castle and draw up the bridge."

"I shan't do that."

"Where and how soon can I see you again?"

She thought a moment. Highgate and Larksmere seemed a long way apart.

"How would it be for you to come to Kingsford next

Sunday morning? There's a good train service, and I could meet you there with the car. I'll bring a picnic lunch for the two of us. Then we can drive a little way, and walk if we want to."

"Sounds wonderful. Wet or fine?"

"Yes. If wet, we can just drive. I would rather meet away from Larksmere." She hesitated, then added candidly: "People do talk so there and everybody knows me. Not that it would matter, but just for the present . . ."

"We'll keep rude hands away from it."

"Just that. You see, I've never minded before, because it didn't mean anything."

"And now?"

Her eyes met his gravely.

"I think it does."

"And so do I."

The waiter brought the bill and they went out into the night.

"I'll call a taxi, Laurian."

"No, I'd sooner walk. There's time. And it's a lovely night."

"How many hours to Sunday?" queried Roy. "Millions, it seems."

"Not so many."

"You can't possibly come up to London again this week?"

Laurian pondered, going over her local commitments.

"Don't see how I can. I'm tied up until Saturday, and then I've half promised to play in a tennis tournament."

"Then will you 'phone me? Not at work. I'll give you my home number. Any evening except Friday."

He scribbled it down on an envelope and she tucked it in her bag.

Hang on as she did to the minutes, Victoria loomed up all too quickly. He drew her into the dark doorway of a florist's shop as they neared the station.

"May I kiss you good night here, Laurian?"

She lifted her face, and he kissed her mouth, then slid his lips over her cheek and kissed her forehead.

"Good night, Roy," she said softly. "Don't come any further. Until Sunday. But I'll telephone."

She slipped out of his arms and was away. She only just caught the train, and when she sat down in a corner seat, she found that she was trembling from head to foot. The woman opposite her, a thin, sharp-featured woman, looked at her briefly, then returned to her paper with a blank expression. The little man in the other corner eyed her for a moment, his glasses gleaming as he turned his head. Then he, too, returned to his paper. Poor things, thought Laurian, seeing them as dim shapes in this blinding new world of hers. They're not really alive.

The train rocked over the points, the blackness outside was broken by lights from the backs of drab houses, and the carriage windows reflected pale ghosts of the three occupants, but one of them was in a land of enchantment far away.

Laurian woke early on Sunday morning, conscious in that delicious moment of drowsiness between sleeping and waking that there was something lovely about the coming day. Then the recollection of Roy came flooding in like sunshine when the curtains are drawn back. What was it about him that had captured her in the first moment of meeting and now had her bound and helpless? He had good looks and a pleasing manner, but so had several others she knew. He was lively, but not fatuous, and beneath his liveliness lay a considerable determination. But personal magnetism was impossible to analyse, she thought. It was just there.

The sky looked grey outside, but it was early yet. She jumped out of bed and skipped along to the bathroom to turn the water on.

She had already been waiting in the dining-room for some minutes when Miss Pennally brought in the coffee.

"Good morning, Penny."

"Good morning, my dear. You're unusually prompt."

"M'm. Got a date."

"You're not going out to-day?"

"Yes. Why not?"

"It's your grandfather's eightieth birthday. You hadn't forgotten, had you?"

Laurian lifted her hand to her mouth, dismayed.

"Oh heavens, I've clean forgotten it, Penny."

"Really, Laurian! Your uncle's bringing him back to-day and your mother's giving him a little supper party this evening. You must have heard us talking about it."

"I haven't. I've been out a lot this week, and Mother hasn't mentioned it to me, I'm sure. And I haven't bought a present for him! This is awful. You'll have to help me out, Penny."

Elinor Pennally eyed her severely, her mouth tucked in. She was a short woman with a fresh complexion and fair hair which was showing streaks of grey. In build she was slight and her blue eyes at that moment looked fierce. She had been Laurian's Nanny until her charge had outgrown her, by which time she had become something of a family institution and remained as housekeeper and companion to Mrs. Vale. She spoke now with the heavily rolled r's and Welsh lilt which Laurian could imitate to perfection, and with the sharpness which could leave its mark even on the master of the house.

"And why should I help you out because you haven't that thought for your elders which I hoped I'd taught you when you were a child?"

"I'm sorry, Penny darling, I truly am. I adore Grandad; you know I do. It's just that I've been in a whirl this week, and it slipped my mind."

"That's no excuse."

"No, I agree. But will you keep a secret if I tell you?"

"That depends." Penny looked at the smiling face in front of her and relented. "Ah well, maybe I will."

"I think I'm in love, Penny. Now you know that

makes people crazy, and that's why I've forgotten Grandad's birthday."

"Who?"

"I'll tell you when I'm sure. Now darling, haven't you anything in that trunk of yours I could give Grandad?"

"We-ell, there's a nice soft scarf I knitted for my father. He died before it was finished. I could let you have that. Not, mind, that I approve at all. A present's not a present when there's been no thought behind it. And I hope you'll have the grace to stay at home to see the old gentleman."

But Laurian was spared the reply to this by the arrival of her parents. She waited until breakfast was nearly over before she told her mother that she would be out that day, and she avoided Penny's eye as she spoke.

"But, darling, Grandad will be so disappointed, and so will Uncle Adrian. I wanted you to meet them at the station with the car."

"I'm sorry, Mother. I really can't break this date. If I'd known, I wouldn't have made it."

"You can put it off," said her father.

"No can do. It's too late."

"Who is it and where are you going?"

"Oh, just a new friend. We're going for a picnic. Don't go all heavy, Father, there's a pet."

"Do I ever?" he demanded over the *Sunday Times*.

"Not often, dear." She smiled at him. "It's rude to read at mealtimes when ladies are present."

"You watch your own manners and leave me to mine. Still, you might as well enjoy yourself while you're young, I suppose."

"You can get back for supper, dear, can't you?" asked Mrs. Vale.

Laurian hesitated, then gave in.

"Yes. I'll be back. Is Uncle Adrian staying?"

"No. His week's holiday is up. I wish he could stay for a little. He works much too hard."

"Pity he can't get some nice little country parish," observed her husband. "Battersea's no good to him."

"I don't think he views it quite like that," said Mrs. Vale.

Laurian slipped away after breakfast. Elsie had her lunch packed ready, and smiled as she handed the basket over.

"Enough for two, Miss Laurian. I hope it keeps fine."

"Thank you, Elsie. Meeting Joe to-day?"

"Yes, miss. We're going for a picnic, too. I'm off at eleven to-day. Miss Pennally's seeing to everything this morning, but I'll be back for the old gentleman's supper party."

"Well, well, well. This *is* a momentous day. Enjoy yourself."

The lanes were full of the scent of May as Laurian drove along between hedges bright and clean with their new leaves. The whole summer lay before her: weeks and weeks before the same leaves grew dusty and faded, then gained a new brief glory in autumn before their span was over. Life had never seemed so significant, so full of promise, as it did on that May morning.

Roy was waiting for her when she drove up to the station.

"Hullo," he said, sliding in beside her. He took her hand and squeezed it. "All well?"

"Very well. Do you mind being driven?"

"Not at all. I'm in your hands."

She avoided the main road and took the car along narrow, twisting lanes for a few miles.

"I love these sunken Surrey lanes," she said, "especially now, when the beech trees are just in leaf. Do you know this part of the country?"

"No. I'm the wrong side of London for it. A nice little car, this. Is it yours?"

"Yes. At least, I share it with Mother, but she doesn't often want it. I thought we'd park it here," she added, as the high banks each side of them flattened out at the top of the hill and she was able to drive the car off the road. "The footpath over that stile leads down to a stream. It's a nice spot for a picnic. What do you think?"

She switched off the engine and turned to him. He kissed her lightly.

"I think you're lovely. Come on."

Laurian carried the rug and Roy took the basket. They were some time choosing the right spot, but finally settled themselves on the bank with a tangle of alder trees and sallows behind them, and a sufficient length of twisting stream between them and the path to promise seclusion. Laurian gave a contented sigh and hugged her knees. The stream was only a few feet across and had little depth at that point, so that it rippled gently over the stony bed with no more than the whisper of a song. On the other side the meadow sloped up to a beech wood. A gleam of sunshine slanted down across the trees.

"I used to come here for picnics when I was a kid," said Laurian. "I've always loved it. This is the only trickle of water within miles of us, and part of the fun was paddling, of course."

"I remember getting a lot of fun fishing for tiddlers," said Roy, leaning on one elbow and watching her, "but I didn't have such a delightful spot as this for my sport. You know, you're a very lucky girl. I guess you've always had everything you wanted."

"Not everything. I was terribly disappointed at just missing the war. Doing anything useful in it, I mean. I was born a year too late."

"You'd probably have loathed it. The Services, anyway."

"Why?"

"Oh, the regimentation, the going through the mill for the first few months. Not so bad once you're commissioned, of course."

"I shouldn't have minded. I'm not soft, you know."

He picked up her hand and ran his fingers over it with a little smile.

"No? People who've had an easy life often have the

quaint illusion that they wouldn't mind roughing it.
You wouldn't have liked it, my dear. The lack of privacy alone would have stuck in you."

"Did you like being in the R.A.F.?"

"Yes. Once I was commissioned I liked it quite a lot.
But then, it was the first time I'd any money in my
pocket and that was a pleasant change. As a matter of
fact, it opened up the world for me in many ways. I
was lucky, too. I was in Canada for some time, and I
missed the dirty jobs. Only came in at the death, so to
speak. Are you hungry?"

"Starving."

"So am I. Let's eat."

After lunch they lay back on the rug, Roy smoking,
Laurian watching the streaks and pockets of blue in the
sky grow larger as the clouds broke up.

"Do you want to walk, Roy, or shall we be lazy?"

"Be lazy. Do you believe in love at first sight, Laurian?"

"I didn't."

"Do you now?"

"I'm not sure, but I think I do."

He threw his cigarette away and rolled over.

"Shall I make you sure?"

"I . . . I'm so bewildered, my dear. I feel winded. As
though something's hit me and I must get my breath."

"I loved you the moment I saw you," he said
thoughtfully. "I'd never seen anybody so vitally alive
and shining as you when you put down that bowl of
flowers and turned to meet us last Saturday."

"Was that only eight days ago? It's not possible. I've
known you always."

"I knew in that first moment that we belonged.
Didn't you?"

"Yes."

"Why do we talk?" he said roughly, and took her in
his arms.

For a moment she stiffened, unresponsive, as though
hesitating on the brink of unknown waters. His mouth
was hard and urgent on hers, and his hands were not

gentle. Then her mouth yielded and her body lost its rigidity as the first wave of passion she had ever known carried her childhood away.

"Roy."

"M'm?"

"What's the time?"

"Haven't the foggiest. Does it matter?"

She lifted her head from his shoulder and pushed his cuff back.

"Heavens, it's half-past five! It can't be. Does your watch go?"

"As far as I know."

Laurian wriggled her arm from beneath him and consulted her own watch, which corroborated the incredible fact.

"I don't know what happens to time when I'm with you," she said. "It just seems to vanish. I can't keep my hands on it."

He lay looking up at her, his blue eyes mischievous.

"Love me?"

"Isn't that question rather unnecessary?"

"It's the first time you've been in love, isn't it?"

"Yes."

"Odd, that. You're so attractive and you must have met heaps of eligible males."

"Nobody who mattered much. I've had plenty of friends. No more than that, though. Roy, I've promised to be back for supper to-night. It's my grandfather's eightieth birthday. Will you come back with me?"

"Do you think that's advisable?"

"Why not? You see, I shan't be able to hide this, my dear. It's too big. And I'd sooner be open about it."

"You said the other day that you'd rather keep it dark for a little while."

"I know. I wasn't sure how serious it was. It is serious, Roy, isn't it?"

"When will you marry me?"

She stopped and kissed his forehead.

"You see. You must come home and face it."

"You haven't answered my question. I love you and want you, Laurian, and I'm not good at waiting. When?"

"I can't answer that before I've even told them at home that I'm engaged."

"There'll be opposition, you know."

"Why?"

"My dear child, use your head. I'm a mere nobody in your father's factory. I've no money and no position."

"Well, that doesn't matter. It's what you are, not what you have, that matters."

"I wonder if your father will see it like that," he observed drily.

"He will if he knows my happiness is in your hands. Oh, I know he seems a bit tough and materialistic. He is, too. But I can get round Dad. He's a dear, really, you know."

"That side of him hasn't been made known to me. Will your mother be on our side, do you suppose?"

"Mother doesn't believe in interfering. She thinks everyone should manage their own lives, even if they mess them up."

"Very sound, too. All the same, my sweet, do you think it awfully wise to spring me unannounced on a family party? Wouldn't it be best to prepare the ground a little? It'll be a stunner for your father, you know."

"Well, perhaps so. But when, Roy? I can't hide it. It's bursting out of me."

"I propose to buy a ring this week. Shall I present myself next week-end, say, for your parents' blessing? Meanwhile, you can probably do a little spade-work."

"I will. I'll arrange it for next Sunday, if I can. You leave it to me. I'll fix Dad."

Roy had rolled back the short sleeve of her silk blouse and was looking at the marks his fingers had left on her white skin. He stooped to kiss them.

"I've left my mark on you, darling."

"Brute. As a matter of fact, my skin bruises very

easily, so you needn't look so sadistically pleased at the evidence of your manly strength."

He kissed her mouth lightly just where it was tender.

"I rather like to mark my possessions. You're mine, Laurian Vale. Do you know that?"

"I do."

"And I'm not giving you up for anybody."

"You won't have to."

"You wouldn't consider a secret elopement, I suppose? At least, that's what they used to call it in romantic tales."

"And what words do they use for it now?"

"Oh, getting tied up on the q.t., I guess."

"I prefer the old-fashioned terms. No, I wouldn't do that, Roy. It would hurt my parents terribly, and I really can't see the necessity. If we both say we are going to be married on such and such a date at such and such a church, nobody can stop us, you know. We're of age, after all."

"Yes. It would probably save a lot of argument and fuss, though. Anyway, darling, we'll see. But don't make me wait a long time. Putting the brakes on where you're concerned means a heck of a strain on the old system. And it's such a waste of time."

"I know. But don't rush me too much."

"Give me some time limit, even if it's only approximate. Just so that I can mark the weeks off and know that we're getting somewhere."

Laurian thought a moment, then laid her hand on his.

"Whatever happens, we'll be married before the trees are bare. Will that do?"

"Not good, but better than nothing. I'll work you back from that. Shall we go and find some tea or shall I see where else you bruise so easily?"

"Tea, or I shall never get home in time."

She ran a comb through her hair and allowed him to haul her to her feet. He held her jacket for her, and as she slipped into it he laid his cheek on her head and held her against him for a moment.

"I'm so glad you don't torture your hair with corrugations and corkscrew curls all over the place. I never realised how lovely human hair was to touch and look at until I saw yours." He smoothed it with his hand, then ran his fingers up beneath it, lifting it from her neck and letting it fall back between his fingers. "Shining and full of life, thick and yet as soft as silk."

"Penny would say it's all because she made me brush it so mercilessly."

"Penny?"

"Was my Nanny. She's now the virtual ruler of the household. Very fierce, and doesn't recognise the word compromise, but she's a gem. You wouldn't say I'd had an easy life if you knew what I suffered at her hands, though."

"Well, I shall congratulate her when I meet her. I think she's produced for me a delightful wife. Some hikers are bearing down on us. Shall we see if the car's still there?"

They walked back to the low stone bridge and began to climb the path. At the top by the stile, Laurian turned and looked back. It would be difficult, she thought, to find a more peaceful spot in the world. The glittering thread of the stream twisted its way softly between the bushes and overhanging trees that fringed it. A few cows were grazing in the meadow, and one had come down to the water and was standing in it with lowered head and swishing tail. Across the meadow the smooth, grey trunks of the giant beeches towered up, and in the sunshine the young leaves that crowned them shimmered with a tender translucence. In a few hours' time, when it was dusk and the grass was dewy, the rabbits would take possession of the meadow. She remembered how Rob, the old retriever, had been driven nearly frantic by the sight of such hordes and had dived among them, not knowing which one to chase and never catching any because of his divided aims. It had always been the culmination of the day's outing: the sight of the rabbits streaking across the meadow back to the burrows on the fringe of the woods, white scuts bobbing everywhere, while Rob ran in circles in a state of delirious excitement, and she had laughed until the tears ran down her cheeks and Penny began to murmur about getting over-excited. It was years and years ago, but the stream and the meadow and the woods were just the same, and doubtless the rabbits were, too. Only there was no Rob to chase them any more.

"What are you thinking about?" asked Roy, vaulting the stile and holding out his hand.

"That I love this place and that I'm glad it was here that you asked me to marry you."

"Sentimental?"

"Perhaps. Why not?"

She swung over the stile, ignoring his hand, then linked her arm in his. He kissed her forehead quickly.

"Why not, indeed."

Chapter Three

As SHE DROVE home, Laurian tried to decide how best to broach the subject of her engagement. She did not share Roy's pessimism about the probable reception of this news, but she did realise that her father would need tactful handling. Perhaps after dinner tomorrow would be a good time, she thought, if they were alone. She had got thus far when she saw Philip Dallas walking along the lane. He looked deep in thought and drew to one side at the sound of the car, without turning his head. Laurian hooted and drew up.

"Hullo there! Can I give you a lift?"

"Hullo, Laurian. Thanks. I was just going to drop this book in at your house. I promised your mother I'd find her a copy. What have you been doing to yourself?"

"Nothing. Why?"

"You look as though you've been trying to kiss King Kong."

"Don't be an ass," said Laurian, starting the car with a jerk, which was unusual for her.

"Sorry. I shot my little arrow in all innocence," he said blandly, and she flushed as she felt his eyes on her.

"It's Grandad Gordon's eightieth birthday to-day," she said hurriedly. "I promised to be home for the little supper party Mother's giving him."

"Oh, I'd better not butt in, then. Perhaps you'd deliver the book for me, with my compliments."

"No, come along, Philip. Mother and Dad will be delighted. That is, if you can bear a family celebration."

"I can bear it very well, but I think in this case it would be an intrusion. I admire your grandfather very much. He seems an amazingly happy man."

"Yes, he is. I don't know how you can be when you've practically lost your sight, but he is."

"Has he lived with you for many years?"

"Since his eyes began to fail him about five years ago. Dad insisted, but it took Mother ages to persuade him. He spends odd weeks with Uncle Adrian in London. They've just been to Torquay for a week's holiday. Uncle Adrian's had a bad bout of 'flu and the doctor ordered him away, so he took Grandad with him. He should have had a month, of course, but he can't be parted from his parish any longer."

She had been talking quickly, anxious to keep his attention away from her. Now, as she drew near home, she added:

"Well, if I really can't persuade you to come and join us, can I drive you home?"

"No thanks. Just stop a few yards along, by the gate, will you? I can cut across the fields then. I've tickets for a Beethoven concert at the Albert Hall on Friday. Will you come with me, Laurian?"

She hesitated as she stopped the car.

"Doesn't it appeal to you?"

"Oh yes, it does. You see . . . ."

"Well?" he asked gently.

"I think you should know, Philip. A week ago I told

you there was nobody else. That was true. It isn't true now."

"I see."

The silence was broken only by the ticking over of the engine, and Laurian, on impulse, switched it off and turned to him.

"I'm sorry."

"You have no need to be. Thank you for being so honest about it. That's what I love you for, you know. Your honesty. It's ... rare, I think. Well, since we know where we are, is there any reason why I shouldn't have the pleasure of your company on Friday, even if it does savour of a fond farewell?"

"No reason at all. I shall look forward to it."

"Splendid. Shall we say six o'clock at my club?"

"It's a date, Philip. What I've told you is a secret, so far. I'm telling the parents to-morrow evening. So if Mother telephones before then to thank you for the book, don't say anything, will you?"

"Of course not. Anyway, I don't even know who the fortunate man is."

"It's somebody in Dad's factory. You don't know him. I'm not at all sure that Dad will approve. You see, it's been a bit sudden."

"I should say that's an understatement. It appears to have been as speedy as a shot from a gun. But I do wish you every happiness, my dear, and I don't doubt that you're capable of overcoming any disapproval. Only ... be sure, old thing."

"I am."

"Then all's well. Tell your young man not to be so fierce, though. It leads to awkward questions. So long."

"So long, Philip."

She waved as he shut the gate behind him. In flannels and a tweed jacket, his black hair a little disordered by the wind, he looked younger than usual. He had been very nice about it. There was one thing to be said for Philip, you could always rely on his good manners, no matter what hit him. She wondered if he ever got excited or blew up. She couldn't imagine it. Curiously, she had never liked him so much as now, when she had, to all intents and purposes, dismissed him.

Then she examined her lip in the driving mirror and wondered what she could do about it. It wasn't really very noticeable. Philip had sharp eyes, and he wasn't slow in the uptake, however quiet and leisurely he might seem. An odd person. She'd never really got to the bottom of him, and doubtless now never would.

She put the car away as quietly as she could and crept indoors. A babel of voices came from the sitting-room and she ran lightly upstairs without meeting anybody. A quick shower and a change were essential before she could brace herself to meet the family. Her whole being was so wrapped up in Roy just then that she found it difficult to come out of her private world and face the family relations who now seemed so dim and remote.

The clock in the hall chimed the three-quarters as she was wriggling into a green silk dress. She began to make her mouth up discreetly, and managed to hide the faint swelling on her upper lip. A little powder, a comb through her hair, her pearls, and she was ready for the fray. Penny had left the scarf on her bed. It was soft and fleecy, and Laurian picked it up with a sense of guilt. Being in love was demoralising in some ways, she feared. She arrived downstairs with five minutes to spare before the supper gong. As she opened the door, there was a sudden lull.

"Good evening, everybody." She was beside her grandfather's chair in a flash, and was kissing him. "Many happy returns of the day, Grandad. How well you're looking."

And, greeting over, everybody was talking nineteen to the dozen again, and Laurian was absorbed in the mêlé. At supper, sandwiched between Uncle Adrian and Penny, she surveyed the family with detached amusement. They really were an odd collection, she thought. Her grandfather was perhaps the most distinguished-looking person there, with his white hair and finely chiselled features. He was tall and stooped at the shoulders, and his skin had a transparent look. There was a dry brittleness about him, as though a strong wind would cause him to crumple up into tiny pieces. Her father, sitting next to him, looked twice as tough as usual in contrast: a bull terrier beside a greyhound. All her father's side of the family possessed the same florid, robust air. It was her mother's side which produced the more delicate strain.

Laurian's eyes moved on to her Aunt Miriam, her father's sister, a big, round-faced woman, with rosy cheeks and prominent blue eyes, who always knew best and who was appallingly self-righteous under her air of *bonbomie*. Laurian did not like her, and felt sorry for her quiet, inoffensive husband and her two sons. If she had to translate Aunt Miriam into canine form, she would be a bright-eyed boxer whose attention was always straying to other dogs' bones. And then, of course, there was Uncle Maurice, with all of her father's doggedness but little of his intelligence. Still, he was rather a pet, Uncle Maurice, and his devotion to his wife was quite touching even though it caused the family acute exasperation or amusement, according to their several natures. A rather stupid, devoted old labrador was the best she could do for Uncle Maurice.

"And what is my godchild thinking about?"

Laurian turned with a smile.

"Sorry, Uncle Adrian. I was being very wicked and sizing up the family in terms of dogs. Surprising what a wide range we have."

"And what, may I ask, am I?"

"Oh, you're a kind, sagacious retriever. Seriously, don't you think we're a queer collection?"

"Most families could say the same, my child. I must admit that we have some strongly conflicting forces here, though," he added as Aunt Miriam's voice rose above the others.

"Bosh, Enid. You're no more delicate than the rest of us. It's a good pose, though, to get you out of doing what you don't want to do."

"Really, Miriam," began Maurice Vale.

"How much pleasanter we'd be," broke in old Mr. Gordon, "if we'd all mastered that art. I find that doing things I don't want to do has a sadly degenerating effect on my character, and I've noticed the same in others."

"We're off!" murmured Laurian as Aunt Miriam lifted her chin and embarked on a discourse concerning the desirability of fair shares for all where unpleasant duties were concerned.

"I wonder if you would do something for me, Laurian?" said her uncle.

"Of course. Anything. You know that," she replied quickly.

"Thank you, dear, but don't be too impulsive. It's a little proposition that occurred to me while I was away. My Youth Club is flagging lately. I'm losing members, and I've been trying to think of some strong counter-attraction to the cinemas and fun fairs and street corners. It occurred to me that some sort of dancing class might go down well. Not modern dancing. Something with more go in it. Country dancing or this old-time dancing that's getting so popular."

"Sounds a good proposition to me. Where do I come in?"

"Well, we've very little money, as usual, and we can't afford to pay a teacher. I can only make a small charge if it's to attract them, and we shall probably have to pay a pianist and give the caretaker something extra for his trouble. I wondered if you would take on the job of teaching?"

"Gladly. One evening a week?"

"Yes. Just a couple of hours or so. We'd be pleased to put you up for the night if it would help."

"Oh, I can get home easily enough."

"I'd be very grateful. You see, you're young and attractive, and you'll know how to make them enjoy themselves. We have to avoid any suggestion of stuffiness at all costs. And any active recreation is so much better for them than hanging about the streets or gaping at some rubbishy film. I don't think your father will have any objection, will he?"

"Not if you propose it. He has a great respect for the Gordons, even if they are fools where money is concerned."

"You know," said her uncle with a little smile, "your father handles me as uneasily and carefully as he would a bomb, which always strikes me as so odd."

"He's the same with the doctor," said Laurian, chuckling. "He longs to dismiss him as a fool, and sometimes does, but he casts an anxious eye at him now and again because of a lurking fear that perhaps doctors really have got something. He mistrusts the meddling of specialists, whether it's bodies or souls they're concerned with, but now and again a little arrow of uncertainty pricks his scorn of them."

"You've inherited some of his shrewdness, I see. Happy the father who isn't seen through by his children."

"H'm. That doesn't mean to say Papa is not quite a force in the land, seen through or not," observed Laurian, eyeing her father thoughtfully and wondering just how he would take her news the next day.

Her uncle, watching her, thought how vivid and warm a personality this niece of his had. She seemed to bring a shaft of light into this assembly of the middle-aged and the old, making them look dusty and stained, reminding him of the toll which the years exacted. He did not want his youth back, only the courage and high hopes of youth.

Laurian's high hopes suffered a severe quenching the next day, however. As soon as she saw the incredulity on her father's vace, she feared the worst. He put down the coffee-cup from which he had been about to drink, and said slowly:

"Is this a joke?"

"No, dear. It's true."

"But . . . but it can't be. Do you mean that young fellow who was down here last week?"

"Yes."

"You're in love with him?"

"Yes."

"Don't talk nonsense! Why, you don't know him. Or had you met him before?"

"No. It was love at first sight. I know it sounds silly . . ."

"Love at first sight! There's no such thing. Look here, my dear, if this is a joke, it's gone far enough. You're worrying your mother."

Mrs. Vale looked at her daughter closely, and said:

"You've been meeting him this week, then?"

"Yes. I saw him in London on Tuesday, and I was with him yesterday."

"But, my dear," said her father, "you can't seriously mean . . ."

"Listen. People have been known to fall in love at first sight," said Laurian desperately. "That is what has happened with Roy Brenver and me. We love each other. We're going to be engaged. We're going to be married. However difficult you may find that to believe, it's true."

"You're mad," he said decisively.

"Perhaps. But it's the loveliest thing that's ever happened to me."

"How can you possibly know anybody after three meetings? Tell me that," he demanded, waving his wife into silence.

"Instinct. We knew as soon as we saw each other."

"Instinct!" he groaned. "Why, I'd hardly trust a man with a parcel on such short acquaintance, let alone my life! Laurian, my dear, what are you thinking of? I can't believe that a daughter of mine can lose her head so ridiculously."

"I was afraid you wouldn't understand. Don't you think it would be wiser to try to get to know Roy better instead of just opposing it blindly?"

He got up suddenly and walked across to the window. His wife prayed that he might throttle the temper which she knew was rising in him. It would be fatal if he didn't. He stood there with his back to them, his hands clasped tightly behind him, his shoulders hunched.

When at last he spoke, she was thankful for the calmness of his voice, and realised that he, too, had seen the danger.

"Yes, Laurian, I certainly think that it is desirable for all parties concerned to get to know each other better. I hope you will at least have a long engagement to that end."

"I've promised to marry Roy before the winter," said Laurian steadily. "He wants it sooner."

"Then he must have means other than the salary he gets from us, for he only holds a junior position, as you know."

"I was waiting for that point to crop up. You always see things in terms of money, Dad. It's not all that important, you know."

"Perhaps not. But no man has any right to ask a girl to marry him unless he can provide for her. As I don't know much about Brenver, however, I am willing to admit that he may be in such a position. That we shall discover. Meanwhile, perhaps you'll invite him to discuss the matter with me."

"You don't have to submit him to a means test, Dad. I know he's not well off, but that doesn't matter."

"Does that mean that I am expected to finance this venture?"

"No. I'm quite ready to live in one room, if need be, and go to work myself, if we can be together."

"You may be, because you're entirely ignorant of what it means to be poor, but has Brenver the same independent outlook?"

"You think he's marrying me for your money?"

Once again he read the danger signals in his daughter's eyes, and changed course.

"I don't know, my dear. I'm only asking for an opportunity to get to know the man who proposes to take away the daughter who means so much to us. Is that unreasonable?"

"No. But, Dad, don't be prejudiced because he's poor."

"All we care about is your happiness, dear. Will you promise me one thing?"

"What?"

"Not on any account to marry him before six months are up."

Laurian thought quickly. That would just allow her to keep her promise to Roy.

"It's not much to ask, Laurian. I think it would have been more considerate of you to have consulted us, and not have presented us with a cut and dried plan. However, let that pass. You're only just twenty-three, and you have known Brenver one week. Is it too much to ask for six months before you leave us and tie your life to his?"

"No, dear, of course not. It's just that we're so terribly in love, that's all. But I promise to wait until we've been engaged six months, and we start from this week."

"I've your word, however persuasive Brenver may be?"

"You've my word. Now do cheer up. You were longing to get me married last week. Now you're mad about it. I know you'll like Roy when you know him."

"I hope so, my dear. Bring him along next weekend. I shall be away in Worcester for the rest of this week. Now I've some letters to write. I'll leave you to talk this over with your mother."

Laurian turned to her mother as the door closed behind him.

"I'm afraid this is an awful blow to Dad. He'd so set his heart on the Dallas social scale."

"Don't be unfair, Laurian. He accepted your refusal of Philip pretty well, I thought. He only has your happiness at heart, after all."

"Yes, but he's a snob, Mummy. He's always boasting about being a self-made man and starting from nothing, and he's right to be proud of it, but why all this reverence for position and money where I'm concerned? If he could start the hard way, why can't I?"

"Because you've not been brought up to it as he was. Besides, he's always had cast-iron principles about a man's responsibilities, and they include providing for his womenfolk. That's why we didn't marry sooner. Your father supported his mother and Maurice and Miriam. They were desperately poor. Their father died when John was ten and Miriam was only a year old. He went to work when he was eleven to help his mother keep the family going, and he worked like a slave from then on. We didn't marry until he was thirty, by which time he'd bought the little house his mother lived in, settled an allowance on her, and seen that Miriam and Maurice were on their feet. We could have married sooner if we'd gone into apartments, but John wouldn't hear of it. I must have a house and a home I could be proud of, and somehow he did it. He would have thought anything less was an insult to me and a discredit to him. That attitude may seem very old-fashioned now, my dear, but you can see how this casual way of entering into marriage shocks him."

"But it's not casual."

"Well, I used the wrong word, perhaps. Insubstantial, shall we say?"

Her mother's voice was quiet and detached, as usual, and through her words ran the little thread of irony which was seldom lacking, which was too gentle to be offensive, and which was more telling than all her husband's forcefulness.

"Oh, always this materialistic outlook! As if there were no other values. What do you think, Mummy? You're not against it, are you?"

"I don't know enough of Mr. Brenver to say, dear, but I don't believe in interfering. I think it's better for people to have to live their own mistakes rather than other people's."

"Well, that's a bit pessimistic, I must say."

"You've rather winded us, darling," said her mother, smiling ruefully. "It will all work out, I dare say. But try to be practical, even if you are in love. You might get Penny to give you a course of cookery lessons for a start."

"What a level-headed mother I have, to be sure.

That's a good idea. I'll start tomorrow. Shall I take her out these three cups of cold coffee and make some more?"

"Do, dear."

When she was alone, Mrs. Vale leaned back in her chair, looking worried. Such turbulent natures, John's and Laurian's, and such a delicate situation to handle. And how could a girl as warm and generous and impulsive as Laurian understand the tough caution acquired by her father in a harsh world of which she knew nothing? He had fought against odds from his childhood until their marriage, and had won, but not without scars; and his victory had cushioned his daughter's life so that such scars were beyond her understanding. She sighed. The outlook was, at best, very unsettled.

Chapter Four

ROY RECEIVED LAURIAN'S report of her family's reaction a little glumly, but they could not be downhearted for long when they were together. The mere fact of Roy's presence sent Laurian's spirits soaring and left her in no doubt that they could overcome any obstacles which confronted them. They walked in the park and they had supper; they laughed and talked and teased and were gloriously happy.

"If only we didn't live so far apart," sighed Laurian when the precious hours had miraculously flown and they were walking back to Victoria together.

"I know. But it won't be for long."

"Where shall we live, Roy?"

"Haven't thought that one out yet. Better wait until I've had that chat with your father."

"Why?"

"Well, once the factory is finished at Worcester, there'll be one or two transfers, I guess. I may be shifted there."

"When will it be finished?"

"In a couple of months or so."

"But we'd be miles apart then."

"Don't worry, ducky. I should take you with me."

"Roy, I've promised Dad that I'll wait six months."

"Darling, why?"

"I had to. It was only reasonable, after all."

He was silent for a moment, then he smiled and squeezed her arm.

"We'll find a way out of that. I bet you can twist him round your little finger, anyway."

"Up to a point, perhaps, but he's a stickler over some things."

"Maybe, but he wouldn't want to see you unhappy, would he?"

"No."

"Well, then. You're of age. We can marry when we like, and he'll come round. I won't go to Worcester and leave you here. That's flat."

"Perhaps it won't come to that."

"Could you stick not seeing each other even for a week?"

"No, darling, I couldn't."

He drew her into the shadow of a side street, and took her into his arms.

"You know, this is what I hate. Having to search for a little privacy, scheme for a few hours alone. Every day I don't see you seems to be a day lost. And who knows how many days we can afford to lose? I may be back in the R.A.F. again soon by the look of things. We don't live in a secure age, my love, you and I. In your father's time, perhaps, you could plan your lives ahead. Now we have no security. We have to snatch what we can when we can. That's why I grudge every lost day."

"I know, Roy. But I've had such a happy home life, and my parents have been so good to me, that I can't just walk out on them like that. You don't grudge the time we're apart any more than I do. I'm only really alive now when I'm with you. But six months will soon go, and we've the summer to help us. I'll spend every moment I can with you. Don't ask more than that, because it makes it so hard for me."

"I shall ask, and go on asking, but not just now. Here, come inside this yard. I want to say good night to you."

In the darkness she took it to be a builder's yard, but whatever it was, it was quiet and concealed, and she lifted her face to his. She knew that time was passing, that she had probably missed her train, but the world ceased to matter in his arms. She had no mind, only a loving heart and an eager, passionate body. This was the only reality; the compass of one man's arms, her only world.

When Friday came, Laurian went unwillingly to her rendezvous with Philip. It seemed a waste of a precious evening which she might have spent with Roy. Unexpectedly, however, she enjoyed herself, and felt a little ashamed of the ungracious feelings she had harboured during the day. For one thing, Philip was a restful person to be with. He made no demands, his manner was easy and affable, and he took charge of affairs in an unobtrusive way which was very welcome in her present state of ferment.

Her response to music, which was emotional rather than intellectual, seemed to be more ardent that evening than ever before. It was as though this new experience of love had heightened her sensibilities so that beauty in any form had a richer appeal and reflected the glowing warmth in her heart. As the final chords of the Seventh Symphony rang out, and the tribute of a moment's silence was followed by tumultuous applause, she turned to Philip with shining eyes.

"Lovely."

His rather austere expression softened as he saw her face, and he smiled, saying, as the clapping subsided,

"Nice to see such a Miltonic reaction."

It was not until he had steered her through the

crowd and had disentangled his car that she came down to earth.

"Do you always drive up to London, Philip?"

"No. Train's quicker. And I don't find London's traffic pleasant to drive through."

"I'm with you. I get terribly exasperated with traffic jams. It's pleasant not to have to bother with trains or driving, though. Idiot! Not a signal."

Philip chuckled.

"You did say it was pleasant not to have to bother with driving, I believe?"

"M'm. I'd better shut my eyes. It's ghastly having two drivers."

She left him to get clear of London without talking much. It was not until they were running through the outer suburbs that she remarked suddenly:

"What was that you said about a Miltonic reaction, Philip?"

"Oh, just that your face reminded me of two lines of Milton's about music dissolving him into ecstasies and bringing all Heaven before his eyes. *Il Penseroso*, isn't it?"

"Yes, I'd forgotten that. It was a wonderful concert. I don't think I've ever enjoyed Beethoven so much before."

"It depends on one's mood, I think. Sometimes he's a little too robust, at others he just touches you off."

"If you could only have one composer, Philip, which would you choose?"

"In such a horrible predicament, I think I should plump for Mozart."

"I guessed it! He suits you. Orderly, fastidious, never running away with himself, perfectly controlled."

"I'm not sure that I like the sound of that. Something prim about it. What would be your choice?"

"It would be a difficult one to make, but I think either Chopin or Tchaikovsky or Beethoven. No, on second thoughts, perhaps I'd plump for Puccini."

"Very much in character, too," said Philip, smiling.

"How are the affairs of the heart? I notice that your engagement is sealed."

"Yes. The family is the only fly in the ointment, but I think it'll be all right. Dad's been away at Worcester this week, and I hope he'll have had time to recover from the shock by the time he gets home to-morrow. He's so old-fashioned in some ways, Philip."

"In what ways?"

"Well, he thinks nobody should be engaged until they've known each other years, to start with, and he goes all early Victorian over money. 'Young man, are you in a position to keep my daughter in that station of life to which she has been accustomed' sort of thing. It's so out of date."

"H'm," said Philip non-committally.

"Dad's got no imagination, that's the trouble. You'd agree that love at first sight is possible, wouldn't you?"

"We-ell, yes, I suppose it is."

"Why the doubt?"

"One can only speak with certainty from experience. I fell in love at first sight once, when I was twenty. Six months later, I couldn't for the life of me believe that I'd ever felt like that about a girl who had a sulky face, a mind stuffed with clichés and an outlook as banal as the worst kind of film. I've never been so rash since. That chap's doing a very good thirty, I must say."

"I'm sorry, Philip. It's rotten of me to be talking like this to you of all people. Forgive me. I find I'm very insensitive about other people's feelings just now."

"Rot. You can say what you like to me at any time. You know that. Anyway, I introduced the subject of your engagement, but I'm afraid, my dear, I can only be a spectator in all this. That is the rôle you've given me, and I don't find it a particularly happy one. But there it is."

And there was no more to be said, thought Laurian, as Philip accelerated and their headlights picked up the studs in the middle of the road so that they gleamed like jewels, and reminded her of the previous night when Roy had slipped the ring on her engagement fin-

ger and she had flashed the solitaire diamond in the
discreetly shaded light of a little restaurant which they
had found near Victoria.

When Philip said good night to her in the porch of
her home, she sensed his unhappiness and felt a little
pang.

"It needn't be good-bye, Philip," she said as she took
his hand. "We can always be friends."

He smiled a little wrily.

"If you need me any time, of course, you've only to
say the word, but I don't somehow think you will.
Good luck, Laurian. Bless you, always."

He stooped and kissed her quickly, and in a few moments she was watching the tail-light of his car recede
down the drive and disappear.

Roy's visit to her home that Sunday passed off very
pleasantly until the evening. Her mother was her usual
cool, polite self and her father gave Roy the blunt welcome which he accorded to all his guests. Aunt
Miriam, who arrived unexpectedly in the afternoon,
succumbed immediately to Roy's charm and for once
Laurian was glad of her aunt's volubility, which provided a useful smoke-screen for any conflicting emotions
among the rest of them. Not that her father was giving
anything away.

She watched him as they sat on the terrace in the afternoon sunshine. Aunt Miriam was expounding on the
high cost of living, but only Roy was attending. Her father had put his glasses on and was reading a par-
agraph from the *Sunday Times* to her grandfather.
With fierce black eyebrows, deep-set eyes and a Chur-
chillian jaw, he certainly looked a formidable proposition. There were deep lines running from his nostrils to
his mouth, which was straight and tucked away. His
high, broad forehead was impressive, and behind it
lived a mind as shrewd and forceful as any Laurian
had met. She was desperately anxious for his approval
and support, not only because she was so fond of him,

but because at heart she had a great respect for his judgment, old-fashioned or not.

If Roy had some disability, she thought, her father would melt instantly, for, severe though he was in many ways, physical disability of any kind roused in him a deep compassion which surprised many people who knew him less well. To her grandfather, he was always the kindest and most thoughtful of men. An active, full-blooded man himself, John Vale could imagine nothing worse than the chains imposed by disease and failing senses, and if he was afraid of anything, it was of that.

She caught Roy's eye as he bent his ear to her aunt, and he winked at her mischievously, bringing a sparkle into her eyes and reassurance to her heart.

Aunt Miriam took her leave after tea, and Laurian drove her to the station.

"Such a charming young man, Laurian dear. And what a surprise you've sprung on us!"

"I'm glad you like him."

"Yes, indeed. Mind you, he's a lucky young man. He's doing very well for himself. But such charming manners! I admire good manners so much. Courtesy's the thing I've always instilled in the boys. It costs nothing, and makes such a good impression."

Laurian smiled, thinking of the tactlessness with which her aunt trampled on other people's feelings like an elephant on glass, and agreed.

"Where are the boys to-day, Aunt Miriam?"

"Gone out cycling with their father. Of course, we can't run to a car, otherwise I could go out with them on their Sunday jaunts. So poor old mother gets left."

There seemed to be no adequate reply to this and Laurian was glad that they had reached the station.

"Now don't you bother to wait, dear. I'm sure you're longing to get back to that handsome young man of yours."

And having made it impossible for Laurian to leave her until she was in the train, Aunt Miriam proceeded to talk long and loudly on the exorbitant cost of everything. How fond of cycling her uncle and the boys must be, thought Laurian, as the train drew out and Aunt Miriam's round, rosy face drew back from the window leaving a merciful blank.

"What did Aunt Miriam come over for?" asked Laurian, meeting her mother in the hall when she arrived back.

"To get some money from your father to finance Tom's musical education."

"Oh. I might have guessed."

And just then her father appeared.

"Mr. Brenver and I have a few things to discuss, my dear. We shall be in the study."

"And I shall be with you," said Laurian swiftly, "if it's about our engagement."

"Very well, Laurian. As you wish."

She perched herself on a corner of the desk in her father's study, and watched with a glint in her eye the subtle way in which her father relegated Roy to the status of a humble employee asking for a rise.

"Sit down, Brenver. Cigarette?"

"Thanks."

"Now, my boy, as you know, I'm a man of few words and I don't believe in beating about the bush. You and Laurian, after the briefest acquaintance, say you are going to be married. What are you going to live on?"

"Our income. What else?"

"Laurian has no income except the allowance which I make her. Your income is, unless you have other sources apart from the salary we pay you, four hundred pounds a year. Can you support a wife on that?"

"It's not impossible, and I hope to improve my position."

"Very likely. Have you any capital?"

"I'm only twenty-seven, and I was in the R.A.F. for four years, so I haven't had much chance to accumulate capital."

"Then you have no right to ask any woman to marry you."

"I think you're a little behind the times, sir. There would be no marriages these days on your basis."

"We can manage, Dad," broke in Laurian. "I shall be quite happy in a couple of rooms with Roy, and I'm not afraid of work."

"You don't know what you're talking about, my dear," said her father, not unkindly.

"Well, let's not go any further with this examination now. We're engaged and we're going to be married in the autumn, Dad. We hope you'll give us your blessing. Meanwhile, I think you might try to get to know Roy better instead of treating him like a child. We live in a different age from yours; you must try to appreciate our point of view. We don't even know how long it will be before war separates us. We must snatch what happiness we can."

"The state of our times is made the excuse for a lot of silly, irresponsible behaviour, Laurian. Every age has had its uncertainties. Anybody would think to hear some of you folk whine that no other age was as hard as this. It's just an excuse for flabbiness. There have always been uncertainties, war, disease and tyrannies. Smallpox was once a far bigger risk to life than the atom bomb, let me tell you. I've no use for self-pity. Shoulder your responsibilities and don't make excuses for evading them. Life's too easy, not too difficult for you youngsters. That's the trouble."

"But I am ready to face the difficulties," cried Laurian. "It's you who don't want me to."

"You may be, my dear. But is Brenver?"

"What do you mean?" asked Laurian quietly.

"No more, and no less, than I said. Is Brenver expecting difficulties, even hardship, or is he expecting those difficulties to be smoothed away by me?" He lifted up his hand at Laurian's angry expression. "Now, my dear, I am not going to allow a slanging match. I have no intimate knowledge of your fiancé. I pass no judgment. But that question must naturally arise in my mind in these circumstances. The whole affair is much too hasty. I can see no justification for an engagement at this stage."

"Well, I'm sorry you feel like that about it, sir," said Roy smoothly. "But perhaps when you realise that Laurian's happiness is at stake, you'll feel differently. I hope so."

And there they left it.

Laurian walked to the station with Roy that night. She was glad to get away from the house, to be alone with him.

"Well, that's over, anyway. We've established our position, and nobody's going to jostle us out of it," said Laurian.

"Don't look so grim, sweetheart. The old man will come round, you see."

"Oh dear, why do people have to spoil things? We've a right to behave like fools if we want to."

"It's the purse strings your pop is thinking of. He's convinced I've designs on them. Don't blame him. If you've got money, you always think on those lines, I suppose."

"Dad does. Oh look, a new moon."

"These woods seem nice and friendly. How long have we got before my train?"

"A quarter of an hour, and it's ten minutes from here to the station."

"What time is the next train?"

"Another half hour. And that's the last one."

"That'll do. Come on."

They slipped inside the pine wood, and Roy took off his jacket for her to sit on. It was very dark, and the pine needles provided them with a soft carpet.

"Shall I make you pay for your father's spurning of this poor nobody?"

"I'm so terribly sorry, Roy. It was beastly for you."

"The worst part was seeing you and not being able to kiss you. Do you love me, Laurian?" he murmured with his lips against hers.

"So much, my dearest."

With the pungent scent of the pines around her and

the sound of the sea sighing in the branches above, she yielded to his love-making with an ardour that left her spent and shaken in his arms. And in the end, he had to run to catch the last train.

As she walked slowly home, she felt tired out. It was so unusual an experience for her that she wondered if she were sickening for something.

Only her father was still downstairs when she got back. He was in the hall winding up the clock. He turned as she came in and was about to say something when the sight of her white face stopped him.

"Mother gone to bed?"

"Yes."

"Good night, Dad."

"Good night, my dear."

He looked after her as she walked up the stairs. He felt helpless and worried. He loved her, yet he could not get near her. She was so young and inexperienced. If only, he thought, your children could accept the fruits of your experience without going through the mill themselves. But they'd none of it. They knew. And God, how little they knew, he thought bitterly.

Upstairs, he found his wife sitting up in bed reading. She put her book down as he came in.

"Laurian been in?" he demanded.

"No. She called out good night."

"I'm worried, Helen. She looked . . . queer when she came in just now."

"Queer?"

"Yes. Used up. Dazed. I suppose that fellow had been making up for lost time."

"Well, I don't suppose they were studying astronomy out there," observed his wife drily.

"Somehow, when it comes to one's own children . . ."

"But Laurian's not a child any longer, John."

"I know. But this is a bad business, Helen. I've a nose for smells, and there's one hovering round Mr. Roy Brenver that I don't at all like. I must talk to Sutton about him to-morrow."

"Interference is a dangerous thing in love-affairs.

Don't you think if you leave things alone, they may work out? Laurian's no fool, even if she isn't exactly worldly wise. I don't think she'd be taken in by anybody who was worthless."

"Not if she has time, but he's trying to rush her. I don't like it, Helen. I don't like it at all."

"Come to bed and stop worrying now, anyway. You can't do anything about it to-night."

"What did you think of him?"

"Too charming."

"Exactly."

Chapter Five

THE WEEKS THAT followed were for Laurian a strange mixture of ecstatic happiness, frustration, and worry. For the first time in her life, she was engaged in a conflict of loyalties which involved her deepest feelings. Had she not been so fond of her parents, she could have ignored their opposition and have assumed, as Roy did, that they would come round after her marriage, if not before. But she could not ride over their feelings so easily, and she knew that her father was not to be so optimistically disposed of; where principles were concerned, he was adamant, and he had attached principles to this question of her marriage. To Laurian it was impossible to see it in any other light than a contract of the heart. Surely a marriage was nothing, if not that. But to her father, it was a matter of duties, responsibilities, money and everything that was cold-blooded, and the chasm between their outlook widened as the weeks went by.

To add to the strain, over and above the conflict with her father, ran the conflict with Roy, whose pressure on her to elope became more and more insistent, and harder to resist, and there were times when the promise she had made to her father seemed a pale thing beside the love which had flamed up between the two of them.

The first day of July was very hot, and Laurian was lying under the beech tree in the afternoon when her mother came out and sat down on the garden seat with her embroidery. She threw her daughter a cushion.

"Put your head on that, dear. You look fagged out."

"I've a headache."

"Can't you ease off a little, Laurian? You're out every evening and all week-ends now, and local affairs seem to claim you all day. You don't have to spend every day at the W.V.S. Centre, do you?"

"I like the work."

"Are you going to be home this evening?"

"No, dear. It's Uncle Adrian's dancing class tonight."

"Oh, I forgot. It's Wednesday. Surely it's too hot for dancing?"

"They're so keen. I did suggest we cut it out for the summer months, but nobody wanted to. I'm glad it's so successful, though, for Uncle's sake. He's so pleased at the good attendance we get. I even persuaded him to polka with me the other week. All the saints are on your side of the family, Mummy, and all the worldlings on Dad's."

"Will you carry on the class at Battersea after you're married?"

"If possible. Depends where we live."

"Haven't you any idea yet?"

"No. Roy thinks he may get moved to Worcester. Until he knows, it's no use looking round."

"But do you plan to rent a house or a flat? Are you getting any furniture together? You seem extraordinarily vague about it, darling."

"I know, but Roy's so unsettled."

Laurian frowned. Roy's delightful assumption that everything was going to be fine was reassuring, but his glossing over of mundane matters like a home and furniture did bother her a little. But that was Roy: ardent lover, but no planner, and she wouldn't change him for the world.

"Well, dear, do remember that you can't live only on love, and that bricks and mortar and food have a part to play. You'd better jog Roy's elbow."

"Mummmy, you've gone over to Dad's side, haven't you?"

"There's no question of sides, my dear. I'm uneasy about your future, but I do realise that you must lead your own life."

"Well, that's something," said Laurian bitterly. "I don't know why you all distrust Roy so. You don't give him a chance."

"My dear, you haven't given us a chance to know him. I've only seen him three times. Why don't you bring him home more often?"

"And watch Dad treat him like a swindler?"

"That's unjust. In any case, you won't overcome his hostility by keeping Roy away from him."

"It's just a deadlock. Dad won't budge—nor will we. Let's not talk about it now. It's too hot to think."

And Laurian closed her eyes. Her mother sighed. Poor Laurian. Her first love was having a rough passage. The marriage of their only daughter should have brought happiness to all of them, but it was driving wedges between them and spoiling their home life. She would talk to John that night and see if she could move him to an easier attitude. After all, Laurian's mind was made up, and they would have to accept it. The strain was beginning to tell on the girl. John and Roy Brenver between them were pulling her to pieces.

Her thoughts were interrupted by the arrival of Elsie to say that Mr. Sutton was on the telephone.

Laurian opened one eye when her mother returned.

"What did the pilot fish want?"

"Your father won't be able to leave early, as he'd planned, so he wants his dinner suit taken up to the office. He's due at some branch dinner to-night. Sutton offered to fetch it, but I said you could leave it on your way. I expect you're meeting Roy in town before you go on to Battersea for the class."

"Quite right, dear. I'll drop it in. Think I'll take the car up. Battersea's an inconvenient place to get at, and I don't enjoy hanging about for buses and trains after an evening's teaching."

"Well, mind how you go. I'd better pack the case, and get Penny to make us a pot of tea."

It was five o'clock when Laurian walked through the swing doors of the building which housed the offices of John Vale Ltd. The doorman recognised her and smiled.

"Good afternoon, Miss Vale."

"Good afternoon. I want to leave this case for my father. I won't interrupt him if he's busy."

"I'll just ring through, Miss Vale, and see."

While the man telephoned from his little cubbyhole inside the door, Laurian watched the comings and goings of the staff with interest. Two girls hurried along with papers in their hands—typists, probably, taking letters to be signed. A small boy, with well-greased hair and a suit too large for him, whistled the Harry Lime theme as he carried a tray of dirty tea-cups towards a swing door on the right. He turned, butted open the door with his rear, grinned cheekily at Laurian and slid round the door with all the aplomb and dexterity of a Ritz waiter. A worried-looking little man trotted across the hall with some files under his arm, passing two girls carrying soap and towels. A snatch of their conversation reached Laurian's ears.

". . . too many liberties, that one. 'I'm here to take down shorthand, Mr. Jarvis,' I said. 'That's all.'"

"Who does he think he is, anyway? Don Juan?"

"Oh yes, three times over. The conceit of it! But then, my dear, all men are full of it, if you ask me."

Their voices died away down the corridor.

"Mr. Vale will be free in a few minutes," said the doorman. "If you wouldn't mind waiting in the reception-room, I'll have the case taken up, miss. Don't you bother."

He showed her into the reception-room and spoke to the girl at the desk.

"Oh, Miss Wynford, Miss Vale is waiting to see Mr. Vale. Mr. Sutton's going to ring through as soon as he's free."

The girl smiled politely and Laurian sat down in a capacious leather armchair. The atmosphere here in London seemed stifling. She wondered if these girls liked working in offices. They seemed happy enough. Odd that all the activities in this building were required for the apparently simple business of packing food into tins and marketing it. Odd, too, to think that Roy spent so much time here, away from her, in a world of which she knew so little. There was no chance of seeing him just then. He was at the factory in the east of London that day, she knew.

Her gloves slid off the smooth silk of her dress, and as she stooped to pick them up she caught Miss Wynford's scrutiny.

"It's too hot for work to-day, isn't it?" observed Laurian pleasantly.

"Yes, it's pretty fierce. This building's cool enough, but Piccadilly at lunch-time to-day was my idea of hell. You wouldn't believe."

"I would," said Laurian, smiling.

She was an unusually pretty girl, Miss Wynford, thought Laurian. Her black hair was curly, and she had a very white skin and large dark eyes. She didn't need such heavy makeup, and there was a jarring note in her voice, but she was certainly striking. She had drawn out some rolls of blueprints and was now trying to hold one out flat while she wrote in a book. She sighed as the print rolled up, and then said apologetically:

"These are the most tiresome things to handle."

"Let me hold the top flat for you."

"Oh, thanks ever so much. Just want to enter the number."

The entries were made and the blueprints stowed

away by the time the telephone rang. Miss Wynford snatched the receiver.

"Yes, Mr. Sutton. Very well." She turned to Laurian. "Mr. Vale's free now, if you'd like to go up. Do you know the way?"

"Yes, thank you."

Howard Sutton was in the outer office sealing up letters when she went in.

"Good evening, Miss Vale. How are you?"

"Very well, thank you."

"Sorry we had to keep you waiting. A very hectic day to-day. Would you like to go in?"

Laurian went into her father's office and found him signing papers.

"Just finishing, my dear. Make yourself comfortable."

Her father's office was an imposing one. It was lofty, with windows occupying almost the whole of one wall and commanding a view of the square with its centre-piece of trees and shrubs fringed with neatly-parked cars. The walls of the room were panelled, the floor was richly carpeted, the huge oak desk by the windows was beautifully carved, and there was a Constable oil painting on the wall. All as prepossessing as money and a good firm of interior decorators could make it, thought Laurian.

Her father pressed a bell on his desk and Sutton appeared.

"That's the lot, Sutton. I shall be here for a bit. I want to study the accountants' report. No need for you to wait."

"Right. Good night, sir. Good night, Miss Vale."

As the door closed behind him, Laurian said lightly:

"Well, after all that, I only wanted to leave the case with you. Have you got it?"

"Yes, thank you, my dear. Sorry to have bothered you, but now that you're here, I want a word with you about Brenver."

She looked up quickly as he went on:

"Information has come to me to-day that has annoyed me very much. That young man has spread the news of your engagement all round the factory and the office here."

"He has every right to."

"Let me finish. You know the new factory at Worcester goes into operation shortly?"

"Yes."

"That means new appointments. A shuffle round. Brenver has let it be known that the chief engineer's post up there is earmarked for him. The whole place is buzzing with it."

"I don't believe it. I suppose your private secretary has dished this up for you?"

"It's true. If he hasn't said so in precise words, he's intimated that his future family connections make it a cinch for him. Now, I want to make this quite clear to you, Laurian. I shall make it clear to Brenver to-morrow. My business has always been run on fair lines. I allow no favouritism, no string-pulling. My employees start from the bottom and work their way up. Promotion gets to those who work for it. I've always had very good relations between staff and management here because they know things are run fairly. There's nothing like string-pulling and edging in relations for cushy jobs to create a bad atmosphere in a business. I'll have none of it. Brenver takes his chance of promotion along with everybody else, and if he doesn't stop this kind of talk, he'll be sacked."

"I see," said Laurian quietly.

Her father went across to the window, and stood there, shoulders hunched. Then he turned to her pleadingly.

"Laurian, can't you see what he's after? He's not good enough for you. I'm not playing the tyrant because I enjoy it. I don't mind him being without money. I'd willingly help him if I saw any signs of him helping himself. But I don't. He thinks I can buy him an easy passage through life because he holds you as a sort of hostage over me."

"How dare you say things like that, Dad, about a

man you don't know, and won't try to know. You've
got this obsession about money, as though everybody is
after it. Roy doesn't care two hoots about your money,
nor do I. We don't want a penny of it."

"Then what are you going to live on? Tell me that.
Has he shown one concrete sign of getting a roof over
your head by his own efforts? You're getting married in
the autumn, you say. How and where are you going to
live?"

"As soon as Roy knows whether he will be working
in London or Worcester, we can make our plans. If we
can't live on Roy's salary, I can find a job."

"And cook his meals and polish the floors and wash
his shirts? What do you know of that way of living?
Where's your common sense, Laurian? In any case,
Brenver has no intention of living like that. He expects
me to pay him a large salary here to be a passenger—
and he's not much more than that now, by all accounts—to buy a house for you, and to make you a
generous allowance. If that's not Mr. Roy Brenver's
idea, my name's not John Vale."

"Why should Roy expect that in face of your attitude?"

"Because he thinks I won't see my daughter lead a
life of squalor. That's why."

"You've no grounds for these allegations, Dad. It's
no use talking to you. You just won't accept the simple
fact that Roy and I love each other, and would be ten
times happier in an attic together than living apart in
all the luxury Croesus could provide. You don't seem
to acknowledge any values apart from money."

"It's not a question of money, but of principles. That
fellow has no principles. It's what that fact is going to
do to your future that is giving me no peace."

"But I must choose my own future, Dad. You can't
do it for me."

"That's what your mother says." He sighed. "You've
had so little experience, my dear."

"I'm glad, if experience means that everything appears in such a shabby light."

"It's not as if you were a weak, clinging sort of girl who'd be happy with a parasite. You've got principles yourself and you can respect 'em in others. You'd never be happy with a man you couldn't respect."

"Dad, when I've proved you wrong about Roy, will you apologise to him, and to me, for all you've said about him?"

"I will. When you've proved it. And will you believe me when I say that nothing would make me happier than to be proved wrong?"

She glanced up at him, and managed a wan smile.

"Yes, I believe you. And I'll prove it."

"How?"

"I shall marry Roy in November. We shall neither of us accept a penny from you, not even a wedding present, ever. And Roy will find employment in another firm. I can't promise you that we'll be able to provide wine when you come to dinner, but you'll find Mrs. Roy Brenver a very happy and proud wife, far happier than Miss Laurian Vale. Good night, Dad."

He had never felt prouder of her than at that moment as she stood by the door looking at him with her eyes bright and her chin high. Then the door closed behind her, and he sat down at his desk and put his head in his hands with a groan.

Laurian was a few minutes late in arriving at the café which was their rendezvous, and she found Roy at their usual table in the corner reading an evening paper. He smiled as he saw her, and her heart sang.

"Hullo, darling. How do you manage to look so cool?"

"I don't feel it. I've come straight from a row with my father."

"About me?"

She nodded and sat down opposite him. The waitress, who knew them, came up and took their order. While they were waiting, Laurian told him of her father's allegations. He listened without interrupting, then gave her a swift grin.

"You know, you'd better leave the handling of Papa

to me in future, darling. You're both too intense about it, and you don't get any further by merely butting each other." -

"But you haven't said anything about getting that job at Worcester, have you?"

"Of course not. But I'm not hiding the fact that we're engaged. Why should I? And if other people put two and two together, it's not my fault. After all, it's not unnatural for a man to do what he can to help his son-in-law. I'll make it clear to the old man to-morrow. Don't you worry, darling."

"Roy, don't underestimate Dad's devotion to principles. He'll never compromise. While he believes that you're marrying me for his money, he'll never come round. We've just got to prove him wrong."

"How?"

She told him. He looked thoughtful, but the waitress arrived at that juncture and he didn't say anything until she had gone and Laurian was pouring out the tea. Then he said:

"You know, you're handling this all wrong, sweetheart. As I see it, the position is this. Your father had set his heart on your making a successful marriage. He'd more or less chosen that Johnny with a title in the family, what was his name?"

"Dallas. Philip Dallas."

"Well, anyway, for snobbish or mercenary reasons, he wanted a good match for you. Either money or family. I don't blame him. You're his only child. Now I've upset the apple cart, being unsatisfactory on both counts. Isn't it to be expected that until we are actually married, he's going to fight tooth and nail to head you off me?"

"Well?"

"Well, as I've said all along, once we're married, he'll accept it and make the best of it and me. Until then, he'll fight every inch of the way. We should have done what I said—married secretly. As long as there's a chance of splitting us, you're going to have the strain of this dog fight. It's wearing you out, sweetheart, and making you and your father enemies. I don't want that. I know you're fond of him, and I know he's fond of you. All this campaigning will stop once we're married and your father realises that his ambitious plans for you are defeated. He won't give in until he's got to, but when he does, he's a big enough man to do it with a good grace, I guess. It's in your hands to put an end to this miserable state of affairs."

"But I promised him, Roy . . ."

"Are you sure that you want to marry me?"

"You don't have to ask that. I couldn't live without you."

"Is there any hope of things improving by waiting?"

"No."

"Then there's no sense in that promise. It will achieve nothing."

"But we've made no plans. Mother was nattering at me to-day about not having a home in view."

"Heavens, who has in these days, unless you've a few thousands to play with. What did she say, darling? 'Now, Laurian, haven't you even chosen the colour scheme for the best bedroom? Pink's warm and cosy. You could make do with one spare bedroom, perhaps, but you really must think about carpets and curtains. Fitted carpets are best, in my opinion. . . .' "

"Idiot!" said Laurian, laughing in spite of herself.

"Now, darling, honestly, aren't your people too pre-war bourgeois for words? Comfort, security, a nice home, a good bank balance—that's all that matters to them. They don't live in this insecure world of ours at all, you know. They live in a smug little world of their them. Do those things matter to you, Laurian?"

"Not a scrap. I told Dad so this evening. They brush aside the things that really matter and substitute the trappings of life for life itself."

"I love you, Laurian. I want our lives to be joined. Marry me and cut clear of all this ugly wrangling. Your parents don't talk our language. They're trying to throw dust and put chains on something that's shining and glorious and free. Are you going to wait while they do it, or strike out for your own beliefs?"

"Roy, darling. . . ." Unconsciously, she twisted the ring on her finger. Her heart, her blood, everything spoke for him. "I must think it over. I've got to go in a few minutes."

"I can fix things in a day or two. As soon as I know, I'll give notice to the nearest registry office in my district, and we can be married the same week. I can take two weeks' holiday, and we can be away on our honeymoon before your folk have digested your letter. You can come back to my digs afterwards until we decide where we'll live. I've a bedroom and a sitting-room, quite big enough for two, and Ma Jenkins, who looks after me, has a soft spot for yours truly and will welcome his bride. What do you say, darling?"

His eyes were sparkling and her own spirit of adventure rose to his, so that her face reflected his excitement.

"No more goodbyes, no more snatched half-hours, no more wranglings," went on Roy. "You'd belong to me."

"Oh, my dear, it would be heavenly to cut and run. I'll see what I can do. I can't say anything definite now. I simply must go, or I shall be late for the class. Not to be torn in half a dozen directions at once—it would be heavenly."

Roy paid the bill and walked with her towards the square where she had left the car. The heat was less fierce now, and the homeward rush had dwindled.

"Do you know, you're looking very lovely. A silk dress and a shady hat—what a bait to trap a man! And then to give me only a beggarly hour!"

"I know. All the time we have together is so inadequate. I never knew love was so frighteningly absorbing. The rest of the world seems an irrelevant distraction and I grudge it every minute. You can't come to Battersea with me, I suppose? The class is good fun, and Uncle Adrian's a dear. You'd like him."

"I'd go through more than a dancing class to be with you, my sweet. Lead on."

And to Battersea Roy went, and seemed to enjoy enormously the spectacle of Laurian as a dancing teacher. Her uncle gave them a warm welcome, and as Roy was a natural dancer, he made a welcome addition to the thin ranks of the males. Laurian was amused at the impression he made on her teen-agers, and a little embarrassed by his keen scrutiny while she was demonstrating.

As always when she was dancing, she was able to throw off her problems and give herself up to the simple joy of co-ordinating mind, body and music. With Roy there as an extra stimulus, she felt a tide of glorious happiness sweep over her, and she knew that she had never danced better. She felt as light as air, and the music became part of her, so that it was impossible to put a foot wrong.

She took the class through the simpler dances which most of them already knew, so that she had an opportunity of dancing sometimes with Roy instead of helping the backward pupils round. As they danced the Valeta together he said:

"You're pretty good at this. Why haven't I come before?"

"I didn't think it would be quite your cup of tea."

"With you demonstrating in a silk frock that curves round you like water—don't be silly!"

"I had an idea your presence might make it difficult for me to concentrate," she murmured as they came together in the waltz, "and there would be a sad falling off in the standard of teaching. You dance well."

"Thank you, teacher. You dance divinely. I shall enroll for life."

"I thought you had already. Right foot, Doris. Start off with the right," she added as the girl in front stumbled in an effort to steer herself in the same direction as everybody else while her feet were inclined to send her off in the opposite direction.

"You like this job, don't you?"

"Yes. I thought I might do some teaching after we're married, to help the finances."

"Bless you. I like your uncle. A much softer proposition than your father."

"He's not of Vale extraction. He's mother's brother, and a genuinely good person, although that sounds awfully old-fashioned. He's not priggish, not self-righteous and not a bit assertive, but just plain good in his soul. Know what I mean?"

"Yes. I'm not a bit good in my soul, I'm afraid."

"Heavens, nor am I! I believe you have to be born like that, you never acquire it. The rest of us just have to go on struggling and floundering. I envy him his serenity."

"I don't envy anybody anything at this moment."

"And nor do I, darling," she whispered, as the dance came to an end and she curtseyed to him with shining eyes.

Laurian rounded off the session with The Dashing White Sergeant, and as she stood on the raised stage at the end of the shabby little Church Hall and watched the lively throng of youngsters putting a great deal of energy and varying degrees of grace into this simple dance, she felt very satisfied. Her uncle joined her.

"A jolly evening, my dear. You've worked wonders with this class."

"I've enjoyed it all immensely. I'm afraid that young man of mine is romping, not dancing," she added, as her eye fell on Roy twisting a girl round with more vigour than was necessary.

"I'm glad you brought him along. When are you getting married, Laurian? In the autumn, did you say?"

"Not quite sure, but very soon. You know I'm meeting opposition from Dad?"

"Yes. Your mother told me last time she 'phoned."

"It's the old story of ideals against materialism, Uncle."

"H'm. Is it really worrying you?"

"Yes. I'm torn between two loyalties. It seems to me that I've got to fail one. I'd like to ask your advice, but

I think I'd better not draw you into the family quarrel. In any case, it's something I must decide myself."

"I thought you'd already decided."

She smiled swiftly.

"I have. But I made a promise to Dad that seems to have become pointless." She broke off as the dance finished and enthusiastic clapping followed. "They seem to want an encore. All right." She nodded to the pianist and the dance went on.

Her uncle stood there viewing the dancers, his hands behind his back, a thoughtful expression on his thin, clean-shaven face with its finely chiselled features so like her mother's.

"Conflicting loyalties. All of us come up against that snag sooner or later. Personal relationships are very delicate, complicated things. The issue is seldom clear cut."

"I don't like hurting people, but after a certain point, it seems that ruthlessness is the only solution. It's all very difficult."

"Be true to yourself, my dear. That's the taper that lights the lamps of peace. If I can help, come to me."

"I will."

Laurian proposed to drive Roy to the nearest Underground station which would enable him to get back to Highgate without any difficulty. As they crossed the common, he said:

"Stop here, so that I can say good night to you properly."

She pulled up by a clump of trees and switched off the engine. Roy slid out and she followed him across the path to the grass beyond the trees. There in the darkness he took her in his arms.

"You're going to do it, dearest, aren't you?' he murmured a few minutes later.

"Do what?"

"Marry me next week."

"I think so. I'll let you know by Saturday. I must have a day on my own before I decide. I can't even

think when I'm with you. I only know I love you so
terribly."

"Does anything else count?"

He was running his hand over the silk of her dress,
smoothing it against her.

"No, darling. Nothing else counts."

"You're not going to keep me waiting much longer,
are you?" he murmured.

But his lips, moving up to her mouth, stopped her
answer.

Chapter Six

FROM THE MOMENT when Laurian awoke with a
headache the following morning and realised that she
was late, everything conspired against her desire to get
away on her own and think out quietly Roy's drastic
proposal.

She spent the morning trying to track down a discrep-
ancy in the Social Club accounts which she thought
would be cleared up in a few minutes, but which
eluded her until it was too near lunch-time to be able
to do anything else with the morning, except type a letter of resignation from the Club. Whatever she decided
about Roy, she could not continue as secretary to a
Club in which she had lost all interest. She had only at-
tended one of the meetings since Roy burst into her
life, and she found it difficult to believe that a few
months ago the Social Club had seemed so important to
her.

The afternoon was unexpectedly commandeered by
her mother on her grandfather's behalf.

"I promised to drive him into Kingsford to buy a
new wireless set, dear. He wants a little portable for his
bedroom. But I've a wretched migraine coming on and
I really don't feel up to it. Could you take him?"

Laurian looked at her mother's white, drawn face,
and agreed. It didn't occur to her that buying the wire-

less set could take the whole afternoon, but it did. To her ears, the four or five models submitted sounded much the same, but not so to the ears of her grandfather, who twiddled knobs and listened with bent head until Laurian wanted to scream.

"I think this one has the sweetest tone, but is it discriminating enough when there's a full orchestra? I think the instruments tend to blur. What's your opinion, Laurian?"

"I don't think there's much in it, dear."

"Let me hear the first one again."

The assistant and her grandfather then embarked on a long conversation about tone reproduction, which led to a demonstration of the latest tone arm for use on radiograms, and then on to the various kinds of needles. By the time they were trying fibre needles on a Gigli record, Laurian gave the afternoon up and leaned back in her chair feeling unusually cross, and ashamed of herself for her crossness. Her nerves seemed to be brittle just now, which was a new experience for one who had never been aware of nerves before. It was this ding-dong fight over Roy that was doing it. And until she was married, it would go on. Roy was quite right. Waiting only made matters worse. She was thinking of Roy's kisses the previous night, and how difficult it had been to tear herself away, when her grandfather laid a hand on her arm.

"Am I being a nuisance, dear, keeping you like this?"

"Of course not, Grandad. I'm very comfortable. You take as long as you like."

"Well, I think I'll have that new-fangled tone arm, young man, if you're sure you can fit it to my radiogram. And a supply of those Stylus needles. Now I'll just hear those portables again."

Poor Grandad. Awful to see nothing but dim shapes: no flowers, no trees, no clouds, not even the faces of those you loved. That was why his ears were so sensitive, perhaps. Some small compensation. And he never complained but was always tranquil and cheerful. The

sort of tranquillity that came with complete resignation,
she thought; with all battles fought, all problems laid
aside, all passions spent. She shivered, her youth reject-
ing this peace that was so near to death. How difficult
to realise that one day she would be old, and Roy
would be old. And their blood would no longer leap at
the sight of each other. How impossible to think that
day could ever come.

Back at home, she found that a particularly loqua-
cious acquaintance had turned up for tea, and Laurian
had to preside over the teapot instead of her mother,
who was by that time prostrate in her darkened bedroom. On and on went Mrs. Draybury, like the brook,
and Laurian marvelled that so much could be said
about so little. When at last the lady took her leave,
Laurian snatched up her hat, told Penny not to expect
her back to dinner and fled.

The common had never looked lovelier. Purple pools
of wild thyme were splashed with the gold of bird's
foot trefoil and made a carpet of oriental richness. Here
and there, the pink buds and creamy flowers of mea-
dowsweet nodded on slender red stalks in response to
every whisper of a breeze. But for Laurian, wrestling
with her conscience, the beauty round her carried no
message.

Everything Roy had said was true. They were at a
deadlock, and the position could only deteriorate as
nerves and tempers became more frayed. But she had
given her word to her father to wait. Even though there
was nothing to be gained by waiting, a promise was a
promise, and to marry Roy secretly would be a betrayal in her father's eyes.

Round and round went the arguments in her head,
and she had still reached no conclusion when her eye
was caught by two golfers walking in her direction. One
was Philip Dallas, the other a man she dimly recognised as the headmaster of the local Grammar School.
They had their golf clubs slung over their shoulders
and had evidently finished the game. As she watched
them, they parted company, Philip's companion turning

off to the left up a track which led to the village. This was too much, thought Laurian. Ill-mannered or not, she refused to face anybody just then. And, diving through some bushes on her right, she virtually disappeared under Philip's nose. Pushing her way along a narrow track overgrown with bramble and gorse bushes, she emerged on to the fairway, crossed it, and took a path that wound through bushes and trees away from the direction of Larksmere.

The sun was sinking and the breeze had freshened when she finally made her way home. The common was deserted, and the only sound was the wind in the long grass around her. She thought how beautiful it looked, rippling and bowing, burnished by the sun's last rays. She felt tired, but she had managed to come to a decision. She could not go behind her father's back. She would ask him to release her from her promise, and if he refused, tell him that she could stand the situation no longer. And, eager to get the issue settled, she decided to tackle him that night about it.

As she rehearsed the words, the gremlin which had sat on her shoulder all day brought her face to face with Philip as she came out into the lane. She looked a little confused.

"Good evening."

"Hullo, Laurian. Are we on speaking terms, or do I pass on my way with a polite bow?"

"I'm sorry, Philip. I just had to be alone to thrash out a problem."

"I see. Well, I'll leave you to it," he said calmly, and was about to walk on, when she put a hand on his arm to stop him.

"You're annoyed, aren't you?"

"My dear girl, you've every right to your privacy, though it would have been a little more gracious on your part to have spared a minute to explain, instead of just bolting."

"I know, but I'd something very important on my mind."

"Quite. Well, I'll be getting along. Good night."

Why this mild rebuke should have had such an explosive effect on her, she couldn't explain, but the incident, trifling though it was, seemed suddenly to be the last straw on top of the strains and stresses of the day.

"If you want to stand on your dignity, do," she cried furiously.

Philip stopped and came back to her. He didn't reply, but something in his thoughtful scrutiny drove her on recklessly.

"You'd never be rude to anybody, would you, Philip? You'd never cut them; you'd never ask a girl to marry you if you had no money; you'd always do the correct thing and never lose your temper. The perfect gentleman, in fact. And too darned perfect, if you ask me."

"But I don't. And I have been known to turn rude children over my knee before now."

She turned aside and leaned over a gate, trembling and absurdly near to tears. She heard the clatter of his clubs as he dropped his bag on the grass verge. She fumbled at the latch to the gate with a vague idea of escaping, but his hand came down on hers.

"You've tried that once before this evening. Now, what's it all about, my dear? Do you want a hanky?"

"Yes, please. I came out in a rush and left mine behind." She wiped her eyes with the silk square which he produced from the breast pocket of his tweed jacket, and said shakily: "I'm terribly sorry, Philip. Made a complete ass of myself. Please forgive me."

"Of course. But why the outburst and upset? Not like you to get in a stew."

"I just felt strung up to a breaking-point, and I broke," she said simply. "I've had a beast of a day, and my engagement is causing such trouble that I'm getting desperate. But that's no excuse for being so rude to you."

"Agreed. But I'll let you off with a caution this time. I met your father in town a week or two ago. I gathered all was not well on the home front."

"The trouble is all of his making. But he's not going

to run my life for me. I'm of an age to make my own
decisions. The silly part is that it's all so unnecessary.
I'm wonderfully happy if only they'll not interfere. But
let's not talk about it now. I must seem a monster of
callousness where you're concerned, Philip."

"No. Only younger than I thought."

He picked up his clubs and they walked down the
lane together. It was nearly dark, and a bat was
swooping between the hedges in front of them.

"Did you have a good game this evening?"

"Pretty good, thanks. I met Dr. Grenville outside the
Red Lion and got hauled in for a drink, otherwise I
shouldn't have crossed your path again."

"Name any penance, Philip, and I'll do it. My head
is bowed."

"The only thing I want from you, my dear, is something you can't give. Being in love isn't all beer and
skittles, is it? Keep your chin up."

And he left her to meditate once again on the approaching show-down with her father.

She ran him to earth in his study, where he was writing out cheques for various household accounts.

"Can you spare a few minutes, Dad? There's something I want to ask you."

"Yes. I've something to ask you, too. Just a minute."

He signed the cheque, clipped it to the account, and
pushed back his chair. Laurian had walked to the window and now had her back to him. He took off his
glasses and closed his eyes for a moment as though
they were tired.

"Well, dear, what is it?"

"I want you to release me from my promise not to
marry Roy before November."

There was a long silence. So long, that she turned
round to see what he was doing, and found him turning
his fountain-pen slowly between his fingers.

"I see. And if I refuse?"

"I think I shall break it, because I can't stand this
atmosphere any longer, and because the promise seems
pointless now. When I made it, I thought it was to give

you a chance to get to know Roy. But you've condemned him without knowing him and no amount of time will change your attitude."

"So you'll break your bargain?"

"I hope you'll release me from it. When we're married, you'll perhaps feel differently about it all. You see, no matter what you say, I'm going to marry him, Dad."

"This is Roy's idea, I take it?"

"And mine. What's the use of going on like this? We're only making ourselves miserable."

"What's the use? You ask me that, when your happiness and your whole future are at stake. You expect me to sit back and say nothing while you, my only child, marry a cheap fortune-hunter."

"How dare you say that."

"I say it because it's true."

"And I'll prove it's not, and I won't wait until November to prove it, either."

"Very well. I see now that there is no chance of our reaching any understanding. I'll make one request, and then I'll wash my hands of the whole business."

"What is that?"

"I want a final talk with the two of you. I'll put the matter fairly and squarely, show you both where you stand as far as I'm concerned, and then leave it to you to ruin your life if you choose."

"Very well. I suppose you want to tell Roy that he'll get no money out of you. It'll make no difference, you know."

"Will you both be at my office at three on Saturday afternoon? I have to be in town in the morning, and it will be more convenient to meet there."

"If you wish. You'll be wasting your time."

"That is my business. I can count on that?"

"Yes. The talk to end all talks. We'll be there."

They faced each other, her face pale and set, her father's grimly implacable. It seemed incredible to Laurian that the great happiness which Roy had brought her could have severed her from her father so completely.

She turned and left him without another word.

The following evening she met Roy outside the factory. They went to a tea-shop nearby, and there Laurian told him of her father's arrangement. Roy whistled.

"What's the old dog up to?"

"I know. He's going to tell you that he won't give us a penny. As if we want him to!"

"He's determined to keep it up to the last, isn't he? He's on the wrong horse if he thinks he can bluff us out of it, though."

"I'll never forgive him for the things he's said about you."

"Now listen, darling. You can't altogether blame your old man. You're the apple of his eye. He naturally thinks you deserve the best that's going, and so you do. With your looks and money, you could have made a brilliant match. Instead, you've chosen a very humble employee in your father's firm. The old warrior's bitterly disappointed. I can understand him. He's got to the top himself, and he's got there the hard way. Like all parents, he wants the best for his child, and he'd like you to start where he's left off. No, let me finish. The disappointment which is making him so sticky will fade once the position is forced on him, but you can't expect him to receive it with open arms."

"You're more generous to him than he is to you, dear."

"The point is, I don't want to be the cause of bitterness between you. Be nice to him, darling, even if he is being a bit of a blight now. It won't last. Now, are you going to marry me at the end of next week, or aren't you, Laurian Vale?"

"I am."

Roy's hand gripped hers.

"You've spunk, I must say."

"When I'm with you, there are no difficulties," she said simply.

"Come along and meet Ma Jenkins to-night. We'd better prepare her."

And so Laurian went to the tall, red brick house in Highgate and met Mrs. Jenkins. The house was one of a row which had once known better times, and which now retained some of its former dignity, although the gardens were neglected, the paintwork shabby, and each house contained several families instead of one.

Mrs. Jenkins was a pleasant, stout woman with white hair and a youthful twinkle in her eyes. Her house was clean and, according to Roy, her cooking was excellent. She held out her hand with a smile when Roy introduced Laurian.

"So this is your fiancée. I'm very pleased to meet you. Of course, Mr. Brenver has told me about you."

"Will you mind my having a wife here until we get a house?" asked Roy, putting a friendly arm round his landlady's shoulder.

"I should mind if she wasn't your wife," said Mrs. Jenkins, laughing. "But I'll be glad to look after you both. This young man needs a wife, my dear. He's a bit of a rascal. You can see how he gets round me."

"I can," said Laurian, smiling. "I'll keep him in order."

"That's what you think, but you'll find he gets round you like he does me. Get along with you. I've some ironing to do. Would you like me to bring you a bite up?"

"Angel. We had a rotten tea. Can you find us a little snack? No hurry."

"I'll bring you some coffee and a poached egg on toast when I've finished the ironing. Will that do?"

"Fine. And a piece of your home-made cake," added Roy, as Mrs. Jenkins went off in the direction of the kitchen.

Laurian followed Roy into his sitting-room, and threw her hat and gloves on to the couch. It was an odd room, being small in area, but lofty in height, and it presented a collection of the old and the modern which was as ill-assorted as a hobble-skirt with bare legs and sandals. The centre of the room was occupied by a round pedestal table of mahogany which belonged to the same period as the horse-hair couch and the marble mantelpiece adorned at each end with a bronze horse. In the centre of the table was a pink glass epergne which housed clusters of artificial sweet-peas. Against one wall was a small sideboard of utility design in light oak, and the chairs pushed in round the table were of the same wood. There was one basket chair which lurched uneasily toward the fireplace, and one shabby hide chair opposite it.

"Not what you're used to, sweetheart, but we shan't be here long. As soon as the Worcester business is settled, we'll see about a house."

"Houses are expensive these days, Roy."

"Can borrow the money, if need be. Don't you worry."

"I don't. But I've told you before that an attic would do."

"But I'm not going to put you in an attic. Stop being so practical and give me a kiss."

"No, not just now, dear. I want to talk to you."

She slipped out of his arms and sat in the basket chair, which creaked abominably.

"Roy, will you leave Dad's firm as soon as you can and get another job? It shouldn't be difficult. Engineers are in demand now."

"Why?"

"I've told you. I want to be completely independent of my father. It's the only way of proving that he's wrong about you."

"Don't be a noodle. You'll both stop this high horse attitude when our marriage is signed and sealed. You know, you've got the old man's pride in you, my darling."

"But surely, after the things he's said, you wouldn't accept a penny from him?"

"For you, I would."

"Roy, I want you to get this straight. When I leave home next week and marry you, I'm leaving my father's money. Every penny of it. I've told him so. And I mean it."

"What a couple of diehards you are! Come out of that squeaking chair, and listen to me." He drew her on to the couch beside him, keeping an arm round her shoulders. "If you both feel the same in, say, three months' time, very well. But I'm not going to commit myself to any promises while you're both so angry with each other. I firmly believe that there'll be a reconciliation very soon. Now stop fuming about your father and give me a little attention before Ma Jenkins brings up the poached eggs."

"But I'll never . . ."

"I said stop."

"You're hurting. . . ."

But he sealed her mouth with his own, and her efforts to resist him died away.

Mrs. Jenkins, considerately clattering the china loudly as she came up the stairs, chatted about Vale's canned foods as she laid the table. For some illogical reason, Laurian found it a little embarrassing.

"She's a bit of a windbag," said Roy when they were alone again, "but she's a good-hearted soul."

"I'm sure she is."

"You didn't mind her knowing about your family connections?"

"Of course not. Why should I?"

"Well, it's none of her business, of course, but she knows I work at Vale's, and when I told her your name, the connection naturally came out. Must say I'm hungry."

"Me too. Being in love seems to have increased my appetite instead of making it languish, as the poets prefer."

"It only languishes when love's unrequited. Salt?"

"Thanks. Do you think Mrs. Jenkins will be heartbroken if I remove those sweet-peas when I take up residence?"

"Shouldn't think so. They're pretty horrible, aren't they?"

"I don't like artificial flowers. In fact, I hate anything that's pseudo. This is fun, isn't it? Eating in a private room instead of restaurants makes me feel that we're already married."

"And is that a nice feeling?"

"A wonderful feeling. Just the two of us legally bound together, and the rest of the world left outside."

"Poor darling. You have had a rotten tussle with the world for me, haven't you? But I'll make up for it."

"You do. Cake?"

"Please. I agree about this being fun. Even just seeing you cut the cake gives an agreeable air of permanence to our relationship. Mrs. Brenver, we are going to have a great life together!"

"I agree, Mr. Brenver."

After Mrs. Jenkins had cleared the table, Roy tuned in to some dance music on the radio, and they circled the mahogany table together, fooling and teasing each other.

She clung to his arm tightly as he walked with her to the tube station, aware of that common reaction to great happiness, a sudden fear of losing it. He felt her shiver.

"Someone walk over your grave?"

"I've staked everything on you, Roy. Hold my everything tight, always."

"Goose! Getting cold feet about to-morrow?"

"To-morrow? No. I wasn't thinking of that."

"What then?"

"A little frightened, perhaps, at loving you so much."

He smiled as he squeezed her arm.

"Well, I'm not going to let that worry me."

Alone in the noisy, swaying train, she thought back over the evening, marvelling at the airy, insubstantial nature of happiness. What had they done? Talked a little, kissed a little, laughed a little, and eaten a modest meal in a hideous little room. And yet it had added up to a quality of happiness which made her catch her breath, fearful of losing something so rare and so lovely. Perhaps it was the stormy passage of her engagement which made their happiness seem so fragile, and which made her long for the harbourage which marriage would provide for it. It seemed to her then as vulnerable to the rough handling of the outside world as the morning dew on the roses, and she would fight for it to the last drop of her blood.

Chapter Seven

LAURIAN OVERSLEPT THE next morning, and her father had breakfasted and left the house by the time she arrived downstairs. Penny surveyed her with disapproving eyes.

"Sorry, Penny. You should have called me again. I only want coffee and toast, and I'll see to it."

"It's all these late nights," replied Penny, following Laurian into the kitchen. "What time did you get in last night, may I ask?"

"Came home on the last train, as usual. It's rather a grey-looking morning, I must say," she added, peering out of the window.

"When I was a girl, I wouldn't have been allowed to come in late night after night. My mother would have had something to say about it if I had."

"But I'm not a girl, and Mother isn't bossy, thank heavens! Did you enjoy your young days, Penny?"

"I was in service from the day I was fifteen."

"That's not an answer."

"And I've too much to do to stand answering idle questions from you. A little bit of bossing wouldn't do you any harm, my girl. I'm sorry you've outgrown my authority, that I am."

"Dear Penny! I'm not so bad, am I?"

"Strong-willed, like your father, but I reckon you're

sound enough at the core. You're worrying us a lot just now, though, honey."

Laurian sighed.

"I know, Penny, but I really don't want to, and it's not my fault. How much coffee shall I put in?"

"Two dessertspoons. Quite apart from anything else, which is none of my business, you'll ruin your health keeping such bad hours and always being on the tear like this."

"Yes, Penny dear. Think I'll put an extra spoonful in. I need it strong."

Penny made an indignant noise, seized a duster from the dresser drawer and departed.

Laurian felt restless all the morning, keyed up for battle and anxious to get on with it. She was meeting Roy in London for lunch, and just before she left, she went into the garden to pick a rose for the lapel of her grey suit. She chose a dark red one which was just unfurling its velvety petals, and as she pinned it to her jacket she felt almost remorseful at cutting short its life, since it was so perfect.

Roy was waiting for her on the bridge in St. James's Park, and, as always, her heart lifted and confidence rushed in at the sight of his smile.

"All set?" he asked, as he kissed her.

"All set. We're going to have an extravagant lunch to-day, on me. I shan't be in a position to say that much longer, after all."

"Attaboy! Lead on."

Fortified by good food and good wine, they arrived at the offices of John Vale Ltd. in good heart. The deserted building seemed to echo as they ran up the stairs. There was always something queer about empty offices, thought Laurian; a suspension of life, a quietus that was unnatural and forlorn.

They found Howard Sutton in the outer office. He blinked his pale eyes at the two of them.

"Good afternoon. Will you go through? Mr. Vale is waiting for you."

"Thank you. Are you so busy that you have to work on Saturday afternoon, Mr. Sutton?" said Laurian.

"When Mr. Vale is about, I'm always wanted. And it's surprising how much work we can get through when we're not pestered with telephone calls all the time."

"But you have a private life to live, after all. I should have thought Saturday afternoon was very precious."

"No. You see, I happen to be interested in my work. I think your father is waiting, Miss Vale," he added smoothly.

"Come on, darling," said Roy, taking her arm.

Her father was standing by the window when they went in, and turned as he heard them.

"Hullo, Brenver. Laurian, my dear. Sit down."

John Vale came back to his desk, pushed some files and papers aside, and leaned back in his chair, clasping his hands. Laurian sat in the armchair, her legs crossed, looking calm and set. Roy sat opposite her, his eyes alert as he watched her father.

"Thank you both for coming. I shan't keep you long. I intend to keep this interview as businesslike as possible, and would ask you both to keep emotions out of it, as I shall."

"Very well, Dad. Before you start, I'd like you to know that Roy and I are getting married at the end of next week."

"I see. Well, I want first to make my position clear to you both, and I'd like you to hear me out without interruption. I've told Laurian, Brenver, and she has no doubt told you, that this is my last word on the matter. After to-day I wash my hands of it."

Roy took out a cigarette and lit it, but said nothing.

"I've opposed my daughter's engagement to you, Brenver, for two reasons. One, because it was too hasty, two, because I suspected your motives. Your behaviour in rushing her into marriage before she has had time to know you, your attitude in the factory about your engagement, and subsequent information about your character have confirmed me in my belief that you are marrying my daughter for the Vale money, which you fondly think I shall shower on you both, once you're married."

He sounded like a lawyer, thought Laurian.

"You don't believe that we love each other?" asked Roy, knocking the ash off his cigarette.

"My daughter is infatuated with you. There is no doubt about that. Laurian has led a sheltered life, as you no doubt realise, Brenver. She has little knowledge of the world or of men like you. In response to your skilled advances, she has fallen in love with a man whose real character, I am quite sure, is unknown to her. No, Laurian, you must hear me out. You may, in your way, Brenver, love my daughter. She is an attractive girl and a very lovable one. But that your main object is money I am convinced, and your character is such that in the end, whether you love her or not, you'll bring her lasting unhappiness. You are the type of young man I most despise. You want a soft life, bought for you by other people's efforts. You're a parasite, with no principles and a great deal of charm. Sit down, Laurian. This is the last argument we shall have, and I insist on putting all the cards on the table. I'll prove my words."

"You can't, because they're lies," said Laurian passionately.

Her father pressed the buzzer on his desk and Sutton appeared.

"Has Miss Wynford arrived, Sutton?"

"Yes. Mr. Vale."

"Bring her in. And stay here yourself."

Laurian's questioning eyes went to Roy as Miss Wynford came in, but his face told her nothing. He was looking at Miss Wynford with a stony expression.

"Ah, come in, Miss Wynford, and sit down. I have your permission to repeat to my daughter and Brenver what you told me on Thursday?"

Miss Wynford tossed her head defiantly so that the feather in her hat quivered, crossed her legs with a nice display of nylons and ankle-strap shoes, and said:

"Certainly, Mr. Vale."

"You must correct me if I am inaccurate in any detail. Miss Wynford came to me on Thursday, Brenver, to tell me that she is going to sue you for breach of promise and she, quite rightly, thought I ought to know the circumstances. It seems that you became engaged to Miss Wynford, whom you met here, just under a year ago. She had inherited at the time a small legacy from her grandmother, amounting to a little over two hundred pounds. Part of that money she loaned to you, and it has never been repaid. Part she spent on odd items of furniture and linen for the home she expected to make with you. She has stored this furniture in the attic of the house where she lodges, and has paid her landlady an extra half-crown a week for this privilege. No interruptions, Laurian, please, from anybody but Miss Wynford until I'm finished.

"With this money, Miss Wynford also paid for her engagement ring, which cost her just on twenty pounds, although at the time, this sum, too, was regarded as a loan to Brenver.

"When, early in the summer, he broke the engagement and told her that there was somebody else in his life, Miss Wynford, naturally very distressed at first, soon decided that if she had lost her hopes of happiness with Brenver, she would at least attempt to recover the money she had spent, by going to court. She has to work for her living, that legacy meant a lot to her, and as far as she could see, she could only recover a very small fraction of it by selling the furniture. And about this time she lost her engagement ring, which was not insured.

"Before taking any action, she told Brenver of her intentions, and he then told her that he was marrying my daughter, that he would then be in the money and would repay her all that she had lost on his account. Miss Wynford thought things over and agreed not to bring the action, and to keep quiet, on the understanding that he would repay her within three months of his marriage.

"This bargain she fully intended to keep, until my daughter inadvertently turned up here last Wednesday and waited in the reception-room downstairs for a few minutes, as I was not free. It was then that Miss Wynford recognised the ring which Laurian was wearing."

"No!" burst out Laurian.

"Oh yes, it was," broke in Miss Wynford. "When you held those blueprints, I had a good look, though I was pretty sure as soon as I saw it. Then I remembered that Roy was with me the evening I lost it. I took it off when I went to wash up the supper things, and I couldn't rightly remember where I'd left it. He must have picked it up when I wasn't looking. And to think I cried hours about that ring, and turned my room and the kitchen inside out, and even had the drain up outside! You can ask Mrs. Thomas, my landlady. We looked for it all that week. And I'd paid for the ring in the first place, and then to see it on Miss Vale's hand, who doesn't know what twenty pounds means to a girl like me. Well, I says to myself on Wednesday night, that's done it. A man who can play a dirty trick like that on a girl, who's no more than a common thief, isn't likely to keep any bargain he's made about paying me back my money. I'm going to court for it, I am. And I'm going to ask Mr. Sutton's advice on how to go about it. And I did. And he advised me to tell Mr. Vale all that I'd told him."

"And perhaps now you're satisfied."

Miss Wynford tossed her head at Roy's savage tone.

"I'm not the vindictive sort, Roy Brenver, and don't think I run after any man when I'm not wanted. Not Doris Wynford. But fair's fair, and when it comes to pinching my ring for another girl, well that's a low-down trick if ever there was one, and I'm sorry for anybody who marries you. You knew I was half frantic that night I lost the ring, and it was in your pocket all the time! You skunk!"

"Now, let's not start a slanging match," interjected Mr. Vale, "though I have every sympathy with you, Miss

Wynford, and thoroughly endorse your words. Well, what have you to say, Brenver?"

Roy shrugged his shoulders, his self-possession unshaken, his face still wearing that stony look which Miss Wynford's entry had evoked.

"I guess you damned me from the start, so why argue now?"

"You damned yourself. But I didn't expect you to shoulder the blame. You don't shoulder anything. I've a proposition to make, Brenver. Listen carefully and decide quickly. If you and Laurian persist in this marriage, you neither of you get a penny from me. You thought that I wouldn't see Laurian endure poverty. You're wrong. Having shown her the sort of person you are, I have done all I can to save her from making this tragic mistake. If she persists, she must accept the consequences. Her home will always be there for her to return to, but it will not be open to you. Her allowance will be stopped at once, and not a penny of my money will either of you see. To do her justice, Laurian has already renounced it, though I'm sure you didn't believe she meant it, or that you couldn't persuade her otherwise. But Laurian shares my respect for certain principles, Brenver. That's why you will eventually break her heart. Now, I've made myself clear on that point, I hope?"

"Quite," said Roy laconically.

"Apart from having a wife to support, you will also have to contend with this breach of promise action. Miss Wynford has a clear case against you, she will undoubtedly be awarded damages, and you will be exposed as a pretty poor figure of a man. The fact that you have no assets makes Miss Wynford's chance of getting the money rather slight, but at least she will have a legal claim on it should your circumstances change. My proposal is this. If you break off all connection with my daughter, I will pay Miss Wynford two hundred and fifty pounds to cover the amount of money she has lost because of you, and Miss Wynford will not bring the action. If you do not, then I wash my hands of the whole unpleasant business and leave you to get out of your own mess. I shall put Miss Wynford in touch with my solicitors, because I think she has had a very raw deal and deserves what help she can get now. What's your answer?"

For a brief second, Roy's eyes rested on Laurian, who sat white and still as a stone image. Then he shrugged his shoulders.

"O.K. I guess you win, Mr. Vale. I'm in love with your daughter, whatever you think, but not with poverty."

"And any man worth his salt," flashed Doris Wynford, "would work like a black for the woman he loved, the same as women do for their men."

"Oh, spare us the heroics, Doris. You're not being exactly altruistic, after all."

"I'm not letting a rotten little twister like you get away with it, if that's what you mean. What use are you to any woman? Don't look so badly, dear," she added, as Laurian came over to her and gave her the ring. "I've saved you from a packet of trouble, believe me."

But Laurian passed by and went out of the room without uttering a word. As the door closed behind her, Roy half rose in his chair, and Miss Wynford said uneasily:

"Poor kid! She's taken a proper knock-out."

John Vale took out his cheque book.

"All right, Brenver. I'll hand Miss Wynford the cheque now. You can go. If you have any pride, which I doubt, you'll send in your resignation as soon as you've found another job."

"Is the sack part of the bargain, then?"

"No, I'm not firing you. I'm not handing you that tool to make trouble with in the factory. I'm merely suggesting that a change is desirable. Engineers are in demand now, and this unsavoury business will not affect any reference we give you, which will come from your immediate superior at the factory, and will relate only to your work. Meanwhile, I think the less said about this the better. Good afternoon."

Roy smiled wrily as he crossed the room and paused with his hand on the door handle.

"You were very lucky, Mr. Vale. The ace turned up in the nick of time for you, didn't it?"

"Happily, yes."

"Well," he said mockingly, "I may have lost her, but so have you, you know."

"Get out."

"Certainly. Good afternoon."

Miss Wynford took the cheque and tucked it away in her handbag.

"Thank you ever so much, Mr. Vale. It's very generous of you, I'm sure. You didn't need to have done it just to keep him from marrying your daughter, you know. He wouldn't have married knowing there was no chance of the money. He reckons his charm's his only asset, and he means to sell it high, I bet. Besides, Miss Vale had had it as soon as she knew about the ring. I was watching her face."

"I didn't offer you the money only to tip the scales, Miss Wynford, though I hoped it would. I wanted to spare my daughter the publicity of the case, in which she would have had to appear, and I also felt every sympathy with you at the way you'd been swindled. After all, you were in a similar position to my own daughter, and had no parents to help you. I know what it means to have a hundred or two behind you. It was many years of hard work before I had as much. Take care nobody else tries to worm it out of you."

"I will, don't worry. Thanks ever so much, Mr. Vale. I hope your daughter won't feel too badly about it."

"All things pass, Miss Wynford. Sorrows, joys, loves. You learn that as you get older."

She stood up a little uncertainly, then smiled as she took his outstretched hand.

"Good-bye, Mr. Vale. I'm ever so grateful."

"You've got guts, Miss Wynford. I admire you for it. Good-bye."

As she went through the outer office, followed by Sutton, she said:

"Who'd have thought the boss was so human! Always been a bit scared of him."

"Mr. Vale is a very fair-minded man. I'm glad he's saved his daughter from marrying that chap. I never trusted him."

"Afraid the home atmosphere will be a bit grisly. What do you think?"

"That's not my business."

"Oh, come off it! Miss Vale doesn't know when she's well off, I guess. What wouldn't I give to be born on velvet! Ta-ta. See you Monday."

And off tripped Miss Wynford, her feather bobbing gaily.

In his office, John Vale leaned his head on his hands, feeling tired. Well, that nightmare was over. And if it hadn't been for Laurian's visit to the office on the Wednesday, he might not have pulled it off. Odd, that such big issues hung on such little things. A dinner date, an unexpectedly busy day, and the call to his wife for his dinner clothes. On such trifles had hung his daughter's future. It made a mockery of his belief that man was master of his fate. Chance. . . . Chance. . . . It had served him well this time, anyway. But remembering Laurian's stricken face, his heart ached for her, and he knew that they had both paid a heavy price in disposing of Roy Brenver. He looked up as his secretary's head appeared round the door.

"Would you like me to fetch a tray of tea from the café round the corner, Mr. Vale? I'm afraid the drop of milk I saved from yesterday has gone off?"

"Thanks, Sutton. That's a good idea."

He walked across to the window and stood looking out on the square, his hands clasped behind his back. The world had gone soft, he thought. That fellow Brenver, now. Young, healthy, yet wanting to buy an easy life from a woman. Hard work, thrift, personal endeavour, all seemed rejected these days. Responsibilities were shelved wherever possible, football pools and dog racing were the main interests. Something for nothing, that was the great idea. And what an idea! That little Wynford girl, though, she had backbone. Realistic about cutting her losses, too. Probably learnt in a hard school. But Laurian had plenty of spirit, too. It would go hard with her, but she'd get over it. You tried to give your child a comfortable life, but it meant that she was less well armoured because of it. You only acted for the best, you always had, but you got precious little thanks for it.

He squared his shoulders. No good getting sentimental and introspective. Facts were facts. He'd saved Laurian from making a colossal blunder, and he'd spoilt Brenver's little game. He'd better telephone Helen, and then get home and see how Laurian was taking it.

He found his wife in the garden when he arrived home. She was kneeling on a rubber mat, a trug beside her, weeding the herbaceous border. Why on earth people got pleasure from such back-breaking pursuits, he couldn't imagine. He had worked hard so that she wouldn't have to go down on her hands and knees scrubbing floors, and now she chose to go grubbing round the garden on her hands and knees instead. Women, he thought, were very perverse.

"Hullo, John."

"Hullo, my dear. Laurian back?"

"No. You didn't say on the 'phone—was she very upset?"

"She walked out on us as soon as Miss Wynford's tale was told. Didn't say a word. Looked pretty grim."

She sat back on her heels and looked up at her husband.

"She's not going to thank you for this, you know."

"She will, one day."

"Perhaps. I wish it could have been less . . . brutal."

"The situation had gone beyond niceties, my dear. She's young. In six months' time she'll have forgotten it. I wonder where she's got to?"

"I shouldn't expect her back yet. She'll want to be alone with it."

But Laurian did not appear for supper, and by the time ten o'clock had struck, they were beginning to feel uneasy.

"Think I'll 'phone Adrian," said Mrs. Vale. "She may have gone to him."

"What on earth for? Hullo, that sounds like her."

The front door shut, and they heard footsteps in the hall. Then the sitting-room door opened and Laurian came in. Mrs. Vale's hand went to her mouth. The girl's eyes looked enormous in her chalk-white face, which was quite expressionless.

"Let me get you a drink, dear," said Mrs. Vale, collecting herself. "You look all in."

"No thank you. I'm going straight to bed." She unpinned the half-dead rose from her suit and threw it into the waste-paper basket. Her clothes looked crumpled, and there was a dirty streak down her skirt. "I only want to say one thing. I don't wish to discuss what happened to-day with either of you, ever. I'd be obliged if you'd bury the subject of Roy, at least in my presence. Good night."

"But, Laurian, darling. . . ."

"Let her go, Helen."

As the door closed behind their daughter, they looked at each other.

"What have you done to her, John?"

"What have I done? It's what Brenver's done, isn't it? I've only opened her eyes sooner than they would have been opened in any case. I don't expect gratitude, but at last you might refrain from sentimental reproaches. None of you women seem to have any common sense. Would you like to see Laurian married to a waster just for the sake of preserving love's young dream for a few weeks?"

"No, but she looked as though all the youth had been wiped from her face for good. Had we the right to do that?"

"Now look here, Helen, I'm about sick of all this woolly-minded nonsense. Laurian's made a fool of herself, and, by a stroke of luck, or to be more exact, because of a girl with guts, I was able to show Laurian just how she was taken for a ride. I did my duty in protecting my daughter from a rogue, and I don't expect to be looked on as a brute for doing it. I now suggest we do as Laurian says—bury the whole business."

"Very well, John. I was only going to suggest that perhaps we all have the right to make our own mistakes, and pay for them."

Which, thought her husband, exasperated, was just the sort of vague, damn' silly remark that Helen would make.

Chapter Eight

LAURIAN CLIMBED UP the slope above a field of wheat, and sat down in the shade of some young silver birch trees. She pulled the letter out of her pocket and looked at it blankly. She had no real desire to read it, and had been within an ace of tearing it up, unopened. Then she decided that she might as well read the last word, though it no longer mattered. His handwriting was neat and rather spidery.

DEAR LAURIAN,

There are one or two things I'd like to say apropos of yesterday's performance before ringing down the curtain.

The first is that my desire for you was genuine. I fell in love with you the first moment I saw you. But domestic bliss on a few pounds a week, my dear, would soon have faded for me, and you too, I believe. A pity the old man wouldn't play—we could have had fun together. But I'm afraid he meant it. Didn't realise that he could be so tough.

If I marry, it is going to be into money. I can't expect you to understand that because you don't know what poverty means. I do, and I don't intend to put up with it. I don't owe the world anything, and I'm all out to acquire from it as painlessly as possible the best it can provide. Sorry if this shocks you, but it's what most people are after, even if they don't admit it. Ideals are all very fine for people like you—you can afford them.

Don't think there's any point in saying more. I wanted you to know that it was you—as well as your money. Sorry I'm not made in the heroic mould, with a "gentleman's" respect for principles. I leave that to people like your father, who's done pretty well out of it, after all.

Don't be too unhappy. Nothing is as important as we think it is. I shall miss you.

Roy.

Laurian looked across the field below her. The wheat was half-way between green and yellow and it gleamed as it stirred in the sun. The spattering of poppies looked like pinpricks of blood. In the hedge which divided the field from the lane, the dog-roses were still blooming. The lane sloped away uphill, and beyond the field of wheat stretched a meadow across which the still shadows of some old elm trees brooded. On the horizon lay the tree-clad Surrey hills, blue in the distance. It was a view which she had known and loved for years, but to-day its loveliness seemed a mockery.

There was a smell of wild mint from the bank where she was sitting. She rubbed a leaf idly between her fingers. It was a long time before she moved. Then she pulled up a root of the mint, and began to scoop out a small hole. Never leave litter about, had been Penny's stern command from Laurian's babyhood days. She tore Roy's letter into small pieces and buried it under the mint.

She spent most of that week out of doors, walking, lying about, trying to come to terms with a world which seemed entirely changed. She avoided her parents as much as possible until the following Friday evening after dinner, when she carried their coffee out on to the loggia and joined them. She placed a cushion on the low stone wall which divided them from the garden, and sipped her coffee, aware that her mother was eyeing her anxiously. Her father was apparently engrossed in the evening paper.

How peaceful the garden looked, she thought, in the soft light of the sinking sun, which had been so generous to them this summer; the summer which had seemed to promise so much. She stopped thinking about that. She had not reached the stage yet when she dared to think back. The iron control which she had clamped down on herself could so easily be breached that way. She watched a bee disappear inside the pink, frilly cup of a hollyhock close by. When it came out, she would tell them. The scent of pinks hung on the air, heavy and sweet.

"Mother, Dad, I want to tell you that I'm leaving home."

Her father put down his paper.

"Leaving home?"

"Yes. I'm going to find a job. I shall stay at Uncle Adrian's for a week or so while I look round."

"When, Laurian?" asked her mother quietly.

"I'm going on Monday."

"I see."

"Would you care to enlighten us a little more?" suggested her father ironically. "Are you going because you no longer care for your home or for us?"

"I'm going because I want freedom to live my own life. It's been said, by you and others, that I have no knowledge of the world, that your money has kept me safe from it. Well, I don't much like the rôle of a helpless cosseted doll. I'm going to earn my own living and live my own life."

"Have you any idea what you're going to do? What sort of work?"

"Perhaps shop work of some kind. Might try to start some dancing classes in my spare time. I'm not qualified for much else. But I shall accept anything that turns up, within reason, whether it's in London or elsewhere. I hope you won't argue about it, Dad. My mind is quite made up, and I've had enough arguments to last me a lifetime."

"I shan't argue. Perhaps it's time you did learn a bit about life. I'm sorry I've committed the crime of trying to protect you from its harsher aspects."

"I don't mean to be ungrateful, Dad, but I've got to get away from here, be independent. I want to make my own life, not have you make it for me."

"Very well. You're of age. There is nothing I can say."

"Will you stop my allowance from now on, Dad? I've a few pounds in the bank to start me off."

"My money's tainted, too, is it?"

"No. I just want my freedom, that's all. I'm sick of people saying—'You don't understand. You've never wanted for anything. You've lived in cottonwool.' I'll stand on my own feet in future. I should have thought you might be able to understand that, as you're an apostle of independence."

"It's different for women."

"Why?" flashed Laurian. "We're flesh and blood, like you. Your idea is to have women pampered and protected by strong men, to look on them as helpless and fragile so that you have the excuse to dominate their lives as you think best. You're hopelessly out of date, Dad, and I'm not willing to be treated like a doll, or to think of your sentiments as noble when they're only designed to feed your liking for domination."

"I've only had your happiness as my aim, Laurian, always."

"Not my happiness, Dad. Your idea of my happiness. But don't let's go on. You understand, Mummy, don't you?"

"A little, dear. You'll come home sometimes and keep in touch with us, won't you?"

"Of course."

Her father got up and walked slowly indoors without saying a word.

"Well," said Mrs. Vale, "I shall go and pick some flowers for the hall. Would you like to clip off the dead flowers in the border for me, dear?"

"Righto." Laurian regarded her mother with an odd little smile. "The garden—that's your port from all family storms, isn't it?"

"Yes. I always find peace in it. Aren't the Madonna lilies fine this year?"

"Lovely. You know, I'd rank the virtue of not making a fuss very high up on the list. And you take a first in that."

"Thank you, dear. You're very unhappy. I wish I could help, but I know I can't."

"No."

"I'll cut some pinks for Father. He's so fond of the scent. Perhaps you'd put them in the little green vase and take them up to him, dear. It would be a good opportunity to tell him of your plans."

"Yes. How is Grandad to-day?"

"Better, but he's going to stay in bed for another day or two. It's strange that he should have caught a chill when the weather has been so lovely. The sweet-peas are not very good. They need a richer soil than this, I'm afraid."

Sweet-peas, thought Laurian, her heart contracting as though the life was being squeezed out of her. Those hideous sweet-peas in the glass epergne. She walked quickly away to the end of the border and began snipping off the dead flowers, wishing that she were dead, too.

It took Laurian a month to find a job that appealed to her and rooms in which to live. The job was in a dress shop in Richmond, and the rooms were only ten minutes' walk away. Accommodation had been more difficult to find than work, for the salary which she was to receive limited the amount which she could pay for rent to a very modest sum. Finally, she had seen an advertisement in the window of a tobacconist's shop in Richmond offering a bed-sitting-room suitable for a gentlewoman, and, smiling wrily at the wording, which she felt should have added "in reduced circumstances," Laurian decided to call at Mrs. Marrowbed's address. It was a tall, narrow house, with clean lace curtains at

the window and a neat front garden. The brass door-
knocker shone so brightly that Laurian was half afraid
to handle it.

A short woman, wearing glasses and a somewhat
lugubrious expression, opened the door. She did not say
very much when Laurian explained her presence, but
led her up four flights of stairs and showed her the
room in question. It had a sloping ceiling, as it was under the roof, but it was large and light, with one window looking out over some gardens, and a smaller one
at the far end of the room framing a delightful view
over tree-tops, with a glimpse of the river. The furniture was plain, but not obtrusively ugly, there was a
faded carpet on the floor, and the divan in the corner
looked new and comfortable. There was a gas-fire, with
a meter beside it. The room, like the rest of the house,
was spotlessly clean.

"There's no attendance for meals," said Mrs. Marrowbed. "I can't do that. I'll just clean the room out
once a week. There's a gas-stove and sink in the little
recess on the landing outside. You can share that with
Miss Woolley, who has the room opposite. She's out at
business all day. If you think it'll suit, it's twenty-two
and sixpence a week and you pay for your own gas. It's
a shilling slot meter."

Laurian investigated the recess on the landing outside. It was screened off by curtains and contained, besides the sink and gas-stove, a small dresser, a large tin
bath, a couple of saucepans, a frying-pan, and on the
shelf over the sink, a jar of bath salts.

"I'd like to take it on trial for a month," said Laurian, thinking that much depended on Miss Woolley.

And so, a few days before she started at the shop,
Laurian moved into her new home, and found that she
had struck lucky. Mrs. Marrowbed, whose manner had
not been at all convivial, turned out to be far better
natured than her exterior indicated. Words did not
come easily to her, and she never talked much to Laurian, but a comfortable understanding was to grow up
between them as the weeks passed. As for Miss Woolley, she was a racy, lively girl who worked as a cashier

in a big store in the town, and who was only too happy to fit in with Laurian when it came to the use of the kitchen.

"Live and let live's my motto," she said as she stood in the doorway of Laurian's room on the first Sunday morning and introduced herself. She was a tall, pleasant-looking girl with thick black hair and a rosy complexion. "No, I won't come in, thanks. That's a golden rule in digs—keep your room to yourself and don't barge into other people's. I've opened the door to some awful bargers, through mistaken kindness, in my time. You lend them a box of matches, and before you know where you are, they spill their life story to you every night, and you have to creep into your room like a criminal and pretend you're not there. You lived in this kind of set-up before?"

"No."

"Thought not. Take an old stager's advice. Keep your little bit of ground private. Just thought I'd have a word with you about the neutral zone outside. What time do you go in the morning?"

They worked out an amicable time-table, and Miss Woolley departed across the landing leaving Laurian reassured, although a little bewildered by this new way of living.

By the end of the week, she was able to take stock of her position. The work in the dress shop was pleasant, and she found Mrs. Frensham, the owner, a likeable, if somewhat bizarre person. The main problem was how to make her money go round, particularly in the winter when, as Miss Woolley assured her, the gas-fire devoured shillings as a sea-lion swallows herrings. She could not hope to increase her salary until she knew the business, and even then she doubted if the business could afford much more. She pondered over this problem for several days, finally coming back to her original idea of trying to run dancing classes in her spare time. She talked this over with Miss Woolley one evening, while they were washing up their tea-things. Laurian's social habits were fast adapting themselves to changed circumstances, and she now indulged in a kind of high tea in the evening after the day's work instead of a dinner, and she and Miss Woolley usually undertook a mutual washing-up to save boiling more kettles than they needed.

"I run an old-time dancing class for my uncle once a week. That's a youth club affair. Think there would be any demand for it here, or would modern dancing go down better?"

"There are quite a few teachers of modern dancing about here. I think you'd probably get more for the old-time stuff. Trouble is to get a hall."

"Yes. I'll make some enquiries."

"My young man's a pianist in a dance band. He might be able to help if you want a pianist, but perhaps you'd prefer a radiogram."

"No. A pianist is best for teaching. I could run one evening class, and perhaps a class for children on Wednesday afternoons. I'll have to take a refresher course myself."

"Well, I'll get a few supporters for the evening class. I like a bit of old-time myself, and several of the girls will come along if they know. I'll spread the news round the departments as soon as you've fixed anything definite."

"Thanks very much. If I can get a start, I'll be all right."

"O.K. I'll get Ted to call round one evening and you can talk it over. You'll have to go into a huddle in Mrs. M.'s front parlour. She doesn't approve of gentlemen callers getting as far as the top landing. It's really because there's a bed in the room up here."

Laurian smiled.

"She's rather a nice soul under that dour exterior, isn't she?"

"Mrs. M.? Yes, she's a good sort really, except for an over-strong respectability complex. After all, you can have fun and games in the parlour just as well as up here, if you want to. But just because you sleep on a divan, but only sit on a couch, the parlour's respectable and the bed-sitter isn't. Quaint, isn't it?"

"Very. It's a question of suggestive atmosphere, I suppose."

"You've got something there. Anything more putting off than that parlour, I've never seen. It's a real museum piece. Dozens of pictures and ornaments, too much furniture, linen chair-backs, a potted palm, and a frightful top-heavy vase of pampas grass on the table. It gives Ted the willies—that pampas grass. He says it's a symbol of frustration. After he'd broken a china dog, absent-mindedly pulled two bobbles off the tablecloth when we were arguing one night and set light to the painted cones in the fireplace with a cigarette, he refused to come here any more. But he'll pop along to see you about business."

"I don't think the pampas grass would help even a business deal. I suggest we meet at a café as soon as I've found out whether there's a hall available."

"Righto. I must fly. I'm meeting Ted at eight o'clock, and it's ten to now. Ta-ta."

It was the morning after this conversation with Miss Woolley that Laurian received a letter from Philip Dallas. She tore it open, not recognising the handwriting, and was surprised when she realised the writer's identity. She hadn't given Philip a thought for weeks.

My dear Laurian,

I met your mother in the village yesterday, and she told me of your move. It was a great surprise to me. I asked her for your address. Could you have dinner with me one evening next week? Or am I cast out with the rest? I hope not. Shall we say my Club, at seven on Wednesday? If you would prefer to meet in Richmond, name a day and time, and I will fall in.

Yours,
Philip.

Laurian propped this against the coffee-pot, and reflected. She had no logical reason to refuse his invitation. She had always liked and trusted Philip, and she had no quarrel with him now. But he was part of the past she had quitted for good. And he might ask ques-

tions, make her think about things that didn't bear
thinking about. Why had he written? Hoping to catch
her on the rebound? She shrugged her shoulders, and
put the letter away. She would decide later. In the end,
she wrote briefly:

DEAR PHILIP,
Thank you for your invitation but I am really too
busy at present to be able to accept. I earn my living
now, you know.

Best wishes,
LAURIAN.

The reply to this came by return.

MY DEAR LAURIAN,
It won't do. The truth, please, as always between us.

PHILIP.

She replied to this straight away:

DEAR PHILIP,
All right. I've finished with the past. I don't want to
dig it up, even for my friends. I'll meet you if you
promise not to probe.

LAURIAN.

And when she read his reply to this, she yielded.

MY DEAR LAURIAN,
My disposition is naturally clam-like, so I appreciate
your point. No probing. Will place my mute self and
car at your disposal on Sunday afternoon at three
o'clock.

PHILIP.

Laurian waited for him at the corner of the road,
which was a cul-de-sac, and as he drew up and got out,
she felt unexpectedly glad to see him.

"Hullo, Philip. Did you have a job to find my hide-
out?"

"No. As a matter of fact, I know Richmond quite well. How are you?"

"Well, thanks. What shall we do?"

"Well, we can drive, walk or go on the river. Or we can go to Hampton Court. Anything there strike a favourable note?"

"Let's go to Hampton Court. I haven't been there for years. I remember the fountain in one of the courtyards used to fascinate me when I was a child."

This suggestion of Philip's turned out to be a happy one, for Hampton Court held no associations later than her childhood for her, and it provided plenty of impersonal things to talk about. They went to see the vine, stood for a long time looking over the iron gates into the sunken garden, walked the length of the border, and finally came to rest on a seat by a yew tree.

"I'd forgotten how peaceful this place was," said Laurian. "Or perhaps peace was something that a child wouldn't notice. Even with a lot of people here, it's dignified and gracious and carries a kind of tranquil nobility."

"Part of our history. A dazzling, if not exactly tranquil part. And now all the passions are spent and we're left with cool courtyards and fountains and flower-beds."

"Yes. But here you're aware of the history, of the past; in a queer way it still hangs on the air. I've never felt it as strongly anywhere else, in cathedrals or monastries or old churches, as I do here."

"Perhaps Henry's strong personality keeps it alive," suggested Philip, smiling. "After all, other kings might only be names in a string of dates, but Henry the Eighth is known as a live and kicking personality to every ragamuffin."

"I'd love to come here very early in the morning, or late on a summer's night, and be alone with it. I should quite expect to see Cardinal Wolsey walking along one of those avenues, dressed in red, looking like Sir Henry Irving."

"We'll do it one day, and see. Am I allowed to ask about your job and your present way of living?"

"If you like," said Laurian lightly.

"Tell me about the job. A dress shop, your mother said."

"Yes. It's owned by a Mrs. Frensham, who is sixty years of age and is a widow. She's an amazing person. Always wears a long, black dress with a high neck and white lace at the throat, has lots of white hair and walks with a stick which has a nobbly top. She's a little lame and I think the stick is useful, as well as impressive. She was in a famous *couturier's* business in Paris, then in a London house before she took this little shop in Richmond. But she left it too late, she says. She's getting too old. Not that you'd notice it. She's shrewd, can be a little fierce, and knows everything there is to know about clothes. She's apt to ramble on about past glories, and I find her very interesting. We have one woman in the workroom for alterations, and I'm the only assistant."

"Any snags?"

"No, I like it. Not very well paid, that's all. But I aim to supplement my income by running dancing classes again."

"Sounds as though you're taking on a busy life."

"That's the idea."

"I think it's a good one. What are your lodgings like?"

"Not exactly luxurious, but comfortable enough. I have a bed-sitting-room and do for myself. Now tell me about your affairs. Have you had a holiday this year?"

"Yes. I spent a week in Nice with my father, then toured through the Alps and finished up with a week in Austria."

"Sounds grand."

"It was pretty dismal, as a matter of fact. The weather was bad in Austria, and I wasn't in holiday mood."

"Why was that?"

"It doesn't matter," he said gently.

Her eyes were fixed on a bed of blood-red dahlias, and he knew that her thoughts were far away. She was only half aware of him, and had completely forgotten that he had ever asked her to marry him. Watching

her, he had the feeling that here was a heart drenched
in pain, quite beyond any human comfort. She could
only find her own salvation, helped by time, and he
admired the courage which she was bringing to the
fight. That was her father's spirit—not to whine when
she was beaten. But he wondered how she would
emerge from the fight. Not unscathed, he feared. The
very brief outline which her mother had given him was
sufficient to indicate the nature of the crash which had
splintered Laurian's world into ugly, jagged fragments.
The only way he could help was to stand by and not
try to pierce the frail, brittle shell she had erected between her and the world. Not yet, anyway. Perhaps one
day, when the pain had lessened, she might invite him
inside it. He felt that she trusted him. That was something. He touched her arm.

"How about some tea, Laurian?"

Chapter Nine

THE AUTUMN PASSED, and Laurian slipped into a
routine of living which gave her little time to brood.
Once the children's class started on Wednesday afternoons, every day except Sunday was fully occupied,
and on most Sundays Philip took her out. She was glad
of his company, yet felt a little guilty at using him
solely as an alternative to the solitude she dreaded. She
was a poor companion to him, she felt. She voiced this
uneasiness one Sunday night early in December. They
had been to a concert and had stopped for a drink and
a sandwich on the way back to Richmond. It had been
snowing all day and the roads were bad, so that there
were few people about and the hotel lounge was empty
when they went in. The waiter pulled armchairs up to
the fire for them, and Laurian held her hands to the
blaze.

"You know, Philip, you should have let me come

home by train. The roads are beastly for driving, and you've got to get back to Larksmere."

"Richmond doesn't take me far out of my way."

"You're too good to me, Philip. And I give you so little in return."

"Nonsense."

"Few people would have been as kind and unde-manding as you've been these past months. And I don't think anybody, with the possible exception of my mother, would have refrained from asking those ques-tions. I'm very grateful, and I wish there was some way of repaying you."

"You do that by giving me your company."

"Pretty poor company often, I feel."

"No. The sidelights I'm getting on life as a shop-girl in a bed-sitter are most interesting, I assure you. And I catch small glimpses of Laurian through the chinks sometimes."

"You're very patient, Philip."

"And very persistent."

"It's no use, you know. I'm wedded to independence for good now."

"All right. I'll be your faithful hound."

"You don't believe me?"

"In your forties, you might be able to say with more certainty that you're wedded to independence for good, but not, my dear, in your twenties."

The waiter arrived with sherry and sandwiches. When they were alone again, she said slowly:

"You're wrong, Philip. I'm never going to put myself in the position of depending on anybody for anything again. Never."

"You're going to be completely self-sufficient. That it?"

"Yes. You don't believe that's possible?"

"It's possible. I've a friend who has achieved it. But he's a middle-aged scientist and his work fills his life. Personal relationships are just like troublesome flies to him—distractions from his work. He brushes them aside irritably. But for you, Laurian? No. You've too much warmth, too much feeling. Where there's sap, you can't stop it rising, you know."

"To my independence, Philip," she said, as she lifted her glass.

"To your happiness, my dear."

"Well, you have been warned," she said, as she put down her glass. "I can't do more than that."

"I never pay much attention to warnings. Are you going home for Christmas?"

The suddenness of this rather took her back.

"No. No, I can't go home."

"Have you been back since you left?"

"No. I've written and telephoned," she added hastily.

"I see."

"You think I should go home?"

Philip studied his glass for a moment.

"I'm not in a position to judge, am I?"

"No."

"Is it bitterness with your father that stops you, or just . . . ghosts?"

"Both, perhaps. But, more than anything, I think, the family relations, particularly my Aunt Miriam. They'll all be agog at my leaving home and Aunt Miriam won't have any scruples at all about satisfying her curiosity. I just can't face their curious eyes, their gossipy minds."

"Are they bound to be there?"

"All the family descend at Christmas-time as a matter of course. It's Father's idea of what's right and proper, and the others are only too willing to fall in."

"I met him in town last week."

"Dad?"

"Yes."

"Did he say anything about me?"

"Well, I don't think he wanted me to know that he hadn't seen you, but he was trying to pump me about you with a casual air designed to make me think that he wasn't out of touch with you, but merely passing the time of day with me. I felt . . . sorry for him."

"I can't. I can't go back. Not yet, Philip. I will, later."

"Do you think it will get any easier for being postponed?"

"It might."

"You're punishing him pretty severely, Laurian. Is it quite fair to make him pay for somebody else's shortcomings, as well as his own?"

"How much do you know, Philip?"

"Not much, and I don't want to hear more unless you choose to talk about it. But I gather that your father was instrumental in breaking your engagement. He couldn't have succeeded without the co-operation of one of the parties, though, Laurian."

"I know. There was a flaw all right, and he hammered on it. But don't you see, Philip, it's not just Dad. I can't go back into that atmosphere again. It's as though I've got a nerve inside me that screams at the slightest approach. I can only bear it by insulating it, and that means keeping away from everybody and everything connected with . . . my broken engagement. I can't bear anybody near it. Even you."

Her face was white and tense, and her hand shook as she picked up her glass.

"All right, old thing. Take it easy. I thought you might be ready to take the dressing off, but I see you're not. Forget it. Only—sooner or later, dressings have to come off, you know. Forgive me?"

"Of course."

But she wasn't blind enough not to know that Philip had succeeded in lifting a corner of that dressing, and had done it deliberately.

During the days that followed her thoughts kept returning to her father, picturing his little encounter with Philip, knowing just how he would look. Her mother telephoned her at the shop the following Wednesday to say that she was spending the day with Adrian and would come along with him to the dancing class in the evening to see Laurian. As she walked towards the hall where she took her afternoon class, Laurian thought again about Christmas, and knew that she couldn't face going home. She just hadn't the courage to meet the questioning eyes, to ignore the tactless tongue of Aunt Miriam.

She found Miss Harper, the pianist, already there, sorting out her music. She was a thin, wispy woman, who seemed to have a permanent cold, and to be wedded to an orange cardigan, the sleeves of which provided harbourage for several handkerchiefs. She was not nearly as good as Ted Bawlesworth, who played old-time dance music for the adult class and who could no more fail to keep perfect time than he could stop breathing, but it was not easy to find a pianist who was free on this particular afternoon, and so Miss Harper had to do. She looked up as Laurian came in, and gave her a watery smile.

"Good afternoon, Miss Vale. A very nasty day. So treacherous underfoot."

Laurian flexed her feet, and agreed.

"How's the cold, Miss Harper?"

"Oh, better, thanks. I've been trying a new cold cure. It really seems to help."

The girls were drifting in from the cloakroom in twos and threes. The class numbered twenty-four, and usually a sprinkling of mothers sat on the chairs round the hall to watch the efforts of their offspring. The children's ages varied from eight to fourteen and one or two of them were beginning to shape quite well.

"You're looking a little tired to-day, Miss Vale," said Miss Harper.

"Yes, I don't feel quite as energetic as I should. Had a longer practice class than usual last night, and a busy morning at the shop."

"Do you need to attend a class yourself? You seem so expert."

"I'd got appallingly rusty, as a matter of fact. Careful, Dorothy," added Laurian, as a small girl skidded over the floor towards a chair and sent it banging against the wall.

Dorothy gave her a cheeky smile and Miss Harper frowned. Then Laurian clapped her hands.

"Come along, children. Line up for the march."

A general scuffling resulted in a wavering line of

black-clad figures. Miss Harper crashed out a chord,
then, to the strains of *Colonel Bogey,* they marched
round the room and the dancing class began. They
needed close watching for the first quarter of an hour
of exercises, which did not excite them, and which they
would willingly have skipped. Laurian's eyes missed
nothing as they went through their five positions, first
with feet, then with arms, and finally both together.
Watching them as they performed to the music, she felt
pleased at the improvement which was beginning to be
evident. She would be able to get up a display in the
spring. Nothing elaborate. Some national dances and a
small ballet, perhaps. She must work it out.

There were signs of joy when Laurian told them to
take partners for an Irish Jig. She usually put that on
early to allow them to let off steam. And so the class
went on, until they finished up with the usual waltz.

"One, two, three . . . *one,* two, three . . . you're out
of step, Gladys. Stop, and start again on the beat.
That's better . . . Don't jig, Phyllis. Smoothly, now. No
romping, Dorothy. You're dancing, remember, not
jumping."

With a few tactful words to one or two mothers,
Laurian watched her charges depart.

"Now for a quick meal and a half-hour's rest before
tackling the class at Battersea," said Laurian.

"How you find the energy, I don't know. But then,
of course, you're young."

And as Laurian engulfed her slender body in a fur
coat, Miss Harper's watery eyes regarded her enviously.

At the Youth Club that night, Mrs. Vale confirmed
that the usual family gathering had been arranged for
Christmas. They were sitting by the side of the piano
on the platform drinking tea during the interval.

"You'll come home for Christmas, dear, won't you?"

"I'm sorry, Mummy, but Mrs. Frensham has invited
me to spend Christmas Day with her."

"You don't want to come home?"

"No. There would be too many reminders."

"Are you still so unhappy, Laurian? I thought you

might be getting over it with so many new interests in your life."

"I'm all right. I haven't much time to think about it."

"Your father will be disappointed."

"Will he?"

"Don't be bitter with him, Laurian."

"I'm not, dear. But he wrecked my chances of happiness pretty thoroughly, and I really don't see that I'm called on to exhibit the grisly remains for the benefit of Aunt Miriam and the rest."

"Do you really think you would have been happy, dear?"

"Dad was determined to prevent my marriage from the first, before he knew anything about Roy. I can't forget that. But this is a pointless discussion, anyway. It's all over and done with. Hullo, Uncle Adrian. I'm going to start off this half with the Valeta. How about taking Mummy? She's dying to have a go."

"You used to be a shocking dancer, Adrian. Have you improved at all?"

"Vastly. Come along and see."

Laurian laid a hand on her mother's shoulder for a moment.

"Don't worry about me, Mummy. I'm all right."

"Yes, darling, so you are. Well, heaven preserve my feet. They're not as resilient as they were once," said Mrs. Vale, gingerly descending the steps to floor level.

Laurian leaned forward to turn down the gas-fire. She was sitting on the hearth-rug, with her back propped against the armchair, and her legs were scorching. She had a note-pad on her knee, and a pen in her hand. It was Christmas Eve, and she was trying to work out a programme for the dancing display. Her eye was caught by the white roses in the centre of the table. They had arrived that morning from Philip. Since flowers were a luxury which she could now seldom afford, she appreciated them the more. He had helped a lot during these past unhappy months, she thought. He had not changed the stony desolation of her heart, but he had helped her to resist being overwhelmed by it, and helped her to keep afloat. And nobody but Laurian knew how desperately she had needed that help.

She jumped at the knock on the door. It would be Miss Woolley or Mrs. Marrowbed, she supposed, as she called out:

"Come in."

It was her father who stood in the doorway.

"Dad!"

"Hullo, Laurian. Thought I'd look you up. Can I come in?"

"Of course. Here, have the armchair. You look cold."

"It's a beastly night." He sat down in the armchair and looked at her a little cautiously. "Well, how are you, my dear?"

"Very well, thanks. And you?"

"Oh, mustn't grumble. I . . . er . . . I brought along a bottle of port and a bottle of sherry. Thought you might like to have a drink in the place. Come in handy sometimes, perhaps."

He put the bottle on the table with a guilty air, and as she watched him, a tiny smile lifted the corner of her mouth; when her father put on his shaggy dog act, it needed a sterner heart than Laurian's to resist its appeal.

"Thanks, Dad. I shall be glad of it. I don't entertain much, but it's nice to have a drink to offer a friend."

"Not a bad little place you've got here," he said, as he unbuttoned his overcoat and looked round. "How much?"

"Twenty-two and sixpence a week, plus gas. I share the kitchen outside with the girl across the landing."

"H'm. Gone up since I was a young man. You know, I paid half a crown a week for lodgings in Stafford once. I had a job there for a year or so. A godsend that job was, too. First decent money I earned, and it turned up just when things at home were pretty grim. My mother was torn between letting me get into the clutches of a landlady in foreign parts, where she was sure I'd get rheumatic fever from a damp bed or starve, and knowing that the money I could send back would keep the rest of 'em from starving. She had an obsession about damp beds, my mother."

He was talking quickly to spare them embarrassment.

"Well, my divan isn't damp, and I don't starve, to prove which I'll cut some sandwiches presently to go with the sherry. Give me your coat."

"Tell me about this job. Your mother says you like it."

"Yes. I'm lucky in my employer," replied Laurian, settling herself on the other side of the hearth-rug, with the divan as a back rest.

He listened attentively as she told him about the dress shop.

"I like it because Mrs. Frensham treats me more as a partner than as an employee. I've a lot to learn about the buying side, of course, but she discusses the financial aspect with me quite openly, as well as any schemes she has in mind to improve the business."

"H'm. Would she be open to a suggestion of partnership, do you think?"

"Possibly. When I've had more experience, perhaps. Anyway, I'm hoping to save a little from the money I earn from my dancing classes with that end in view."

"So you've got that far, have you?"

His voice was frankly admiring, and Laurian smiled as she said:

"Yes. Just. The idea started to grow about ten days ago. I'm doing better with the old-time dancing class than I expected. In fact, I'm getting packed out. The children's class doesn't pay very well, but I enjoy taking it."

"Well, if you want a loan at any time, you know where to come."

"Thanks, Dad, but I've a hankering to do this off my own bat."

"Quite. But it could be a strictly business deal, if you prefer it. You could even pay me interest on the loan."

"At bank rate?" asked Laurian, smiling a little.

"I'd offer you slightly better terms than that."

"Do you usually invest money with so few enquiries?"

"I'm willing to back a hunch. And I've a hunch that you've got enough of my blood to make you a good risk in business."

"Well, thanks. I'll bear it in mind. But I'll have a shot at doing it without borrowing, if I can. That's your blood again, perhaps."

"I believe," he said slowly, "that you rather like meeting a challenge. So do I. Always have. To know the cards are stacked against you, and to win. To pit your own will-power and capabilities against adverse circumstances, and to come out on top. That's living at its fullest, to my way of thinking, anyway."

And how his face showed it, thought Laurian. From the jutting eyebrows to the powerful jaw, he looked a fighter every inch of the way.

"Perhaps you're right."

But you didn't fight battles without getting scars, thought Laurian. This evening she was seeing the victory of one of her fights, though. Her fight for freedom. For the first time, her father was seeing her as an individual, not just as his daughter. He spoke to her as an equal. Even the gift of the port and sherry was a symbol of his recognition of her emancipation. However much he liked to regard women as tender plants to be protected and managed by men, he had now allowed his daughter to enter that select band of people who could be considered capable of running their own lives. It was a notable victory, she felt, and he probably excused it by reminding himself that it was his blood in her veins, after all.

"I'll cut some sandwiches, Dad. You'll have to drink your sherry from a tumbler. We don't run to fancy glasses here."

"Right you are, dear."

He followed her out to the kitchen, and poked round while she made some ham sandwiches. He picked up the bath salts and smelt them, looked inside the cupboard, pulled out the tin bath.

"Do you use this?"

"Of course."

"Pretty chilly for a bath in here, isn't it?"

"I take it in the other room. You don't know what luxury means until you've had a bath in front of a gas-fire. It's gorgeous. Takes all the saucepans, the kettle and the bucket to give a reasonable depth of water, but I manage. Mind that saucepan stand. It's a bit unsteady."

"Your landlady looks rather a miserable soul," he observed, taking off the lid of the vegetable dish on the dresser and looking inside.

"I know. But she's not. She's really very decent."

"What's this?"

"Fish for the cat. My colleague across the landing owns a sandy cat."

"Cats—can't bear 'em. What fish is this, for heaven's sake?"

"Remains of a cod's head. Don't be so nosy, Dad," said Laurian, laughing. "And there's nothing inside that cupboard but suitcases and shoe-cleaning stuff. Here, take these sandwiches, and I'll bring the glasses."

Any awkwardness in the situation had completely vanished by the time they sat down with sherry in hand and the plate of sandwiches on the hearth-rug between them. Her father lifted his glass to her.

"To your success in business, Laurian."

"Thanks, Dad."

It was the right note, she thought, as she drank. Not to happiness, but to success. The one was not on the market for her any longer. A new era had started, a milestone had been passed. Not happiness, but success was now her goal. And if the road ahead looked a little bleak and lonely, she was glad that under the wreckage of the past, she and her father had, on that Christmas Eve, buried their differences without a word.

Chapter Ten

THE HARD-WORKING life which Laurian had made for herself sent the weeks and months scurrying past with a rapidity which amazed her. The old life at Larksmere became a hazy dream severed from the reality of the present by the gash which Roy had inflicted. And time gradually drew that gash together, so that on the rare occasions when she looked back, she was no longer aware of a pain that was beyond endurance, but saw only a scar that might throb a little now and again. It was not a quick or an easy victory, and although she emerged without bitterness, the experience left her with a marked wariness where personal relationships were concerned.

It was this wariness which set the alarm bell ringing one summer morning when she lay in bed watching motes dancing in a sunbeam which slanted across the room. As recollections of the previous evening came to her drowsy mind, she was suddenly wide awake. Had she really been rash enough to agree to spend her summer holiday in Austria with Philip? Surely not. But her memory informed her very firmly that she had, and she could only wonder what had lulled her wits into such a state of quiescence. And pat came the answer: a good dinner, good wine, gay company and Philip's astuteness. The invitation to dinner had sounded pleasant and innocuous enough. He had telephoned that morning to ask if she would make a fourth at a little dinner he was giving to celebrate the twentieth birthday of his young friend, Jill Russell. The other member of the party would be Jill's fiancé, Derek. Laurian, who had been avoiding *tête-à-têtes* with Philip recently, had gladly agreed. There was safety in numbers.

To the dinner, therefore, she had gone, and had enjoyed it immensely, since both Jill and Derek possessed more than their share of youthful high spirits, and their gaiety was infectious. To say nothing of the wine, thought Laurian, gazing up at the ceiling. Her mind went back over the dinner, trying to remember just how Philip had led up to that holiday proposition, for she was sure now, in the clear light of day, that he had planned every move. Ah yes, she remembered. It had started with a casual remark of Philip's about mountaineering. A climbing accident had been reported in the papers that morning. . . .

"And that reminds me," said Philip, "have you two children managed to persuade Grandma to smile on your plans for scrambling in the Austrian Alps?"

Jill shook her head mournfully.

"She won't budge. It's so silly, because she didn't mind us going to the Lakes together last year."

"That was different," broke in Derek. "We went with a party, and we were in England. This time we're going alone, to the Continent, and that one word spells immorality to Grandma."

"Aren't old people difficult?" said Jill, appealing to Laurian. "Grandma's a dear, really, and I hate upsetting her. Besides, if I did she could make it sticky for Derek and me until we're married. But we had set our hearts on going to the Tyrol this year. You see, we're going to begin saving really hard after that to get married, and once we're married, we won't have enough money for holidays abroad for years and years. . . ."

"If ever," interjected Derek cheerfully.

"What with children and everything," went on Jill, "and we'll be too old to climb then, anyway. So it's now or never. Uncle Phil, can't you try to persuade her? Anything you say goes."

"Not anything, my child. I had a word with her about it the other night."

Two eager faces turned to him.

"You did? What did she say?" asked Derek, leaning forward.

"That she'd agree if you went with some responsible person," said Philip, grinning, "but that it wasn't fitting for two young lovers to go traipsing about the Continent alone, and she was surprised at my lax attitude, particularly as Jill is barely out of school."

"Help!" said Jill. "She just doesn't live in this age at all. Uncle. Darling Uncle Phil. I suppose you wouldn't like a holiday in Austria?"

"Not just to play gooseberry to you two. I might if I had a companion. I suppose you wouldn't care to come, Laurian?"

"Me?"

"Oh, Miss Vale, would you?" Jill's blue eyes opened wide as she turned to Laurian. "It would be a really Christian act. And you'd enjoy it. I mean, Uncle Phil's quite nice to be with. And we'd be *so* grateful. We've always dreamed of climbing in the Alps. And it's the last chance we'll have of our dream coming true. Do please say yes."

"It would be most awfully nice of you, Miss Vale," said Derek diffidently.

"Don't you know anybody else suitable, Philip?" asked Laurian.

His eyes met hers guilelessly.

"Afraid not. But don't let these two stampede you into a holiday you don't want. It's glorious country, though. I think you'd like it."

"Spare a thought for the victims of old-fashioned conventions," wheedled Jill. "It's not all fun being engaged when you live with a Grandma like mine."

And against this appeal, Laurian stood no chance. It winged straight home.

"All right. I'm in on it."

Jill clapped her hands excitedly.

"Oh, bless you, Laurian. You don't mind me calling you Laurian, do you? Bless you a hundred times. Derry, we'll climb the Wildspitz together! Oh, what a lovely birthday!"

The girl's face as she turned to Derek was shining with a transparent happiness which brought a queer little ache to Laurian's heart. Derek put his hand over Jill's as he said:

"We're no end grateful to you, Miss Vale, and to you, sir."

But Philip merely smiled as he poured out more wine, and said nothing.

"Will Grandma agree that you are a responsible person, in view of your lax attitude towards the holiday in the first place?" asked Laurian demurely.

"Oh yes," broke in Jill. "You see, Uncle Phil is really my guardian. He's not my uncle at all. My father ... Well, you explain, Uncle Phil."

"I will, if you'll give me a chance, chatterbox. Jill's father was a very great friend of mine, Laurian. He died six years ago, after a long illness, and he made me his trustee and asked me to keep an eye on Jill, who had lost her mother a few years before. Grandma Russell is a grand old lady, but—well, that generation had different ideas about how to bring up children, and a different world to do it in. I just poke a nose in now and again and loosen the reins a bit. Not that I let Jill get away with everything she likes. She's got her father's ingratiating way of talking you out of your crease, and before you know where you are, you find you're stumped."

"Those tactics work with Derry sometimes, but not with you, Uncle Phil. You're crafty. You let me think I've shifted you, then you reveal that your bat's kept contact with the same spot all the time. Derry's much easier."

She smiled mischievously at her fiancé. He was a nice-looking young man, Derek Rockingham, with black wavy hair, dark eyes, a ruddy complexion, and of a compact, stocky build. He was a little on the short side, but since Jill was very *petite*, his lack of inches caused him no inferiority complex. There was an elfin attraction about Jill, with her smooth, fair hair, dancing eyes and pointed little face. The two of them together made a striking contrast of airiness and solidity.

"Easy game, am I?" queried Derek ominously. "I'll settle with you for that when we're alone. Will you take the car?" he added, turning to Philip.

"Of course. We'll have the maps out and decide on the route some time next week. And I'd better get on to the A.A. right away about a passage. Is the beginning of September convenient for you, Laurian?"

"Yes. I can take my holiday more or less when I like. Mrs. Frensham will step in while I'm away. . . ."

And she had walked into it as easily as that. For one moment, she wondered if she could retract. Telephone Philip and say that on second thoughts she couldn't really spare the time from the business. Then the recollection of Jill's happy, eager face made it impossible. She couldn't spoil it for them and she had every sympathy with young love up against authority. But the more she examined her own position, the more vulnerable it seemed. For three years she had been fighting against Philip's determination to marry her. At first, in those unhappy months after she left home, she had leaned on his kindness gratefully, too lonely and hurt to be able to turn away the one small comfort which his friendship had provided. Then gradually, as the busy months passed, she had built round herself a shield of business-like efficiency, concentrating all her energies on her job, until now, by careful saving, she owned a quarter share in the dress shop, and had undertaken its management when failing health had caused Mrs. Frensham to step back into semi-retirement. But Philip's siege had continued, and lately she had felt that the rôle of independent business woman which she had undertaken was being slowly undermined. She had therefore carefully, without wishing to hurt him, withdrawn a little, making the business her excuse for not being able to meet him very often, and ensuring that the tone of the meetings which did take place remained briskly impersonal.

And now, of all lunatic things to do, she had agreed to make a fourth on a holiday jaunt, where it would be quite impossible to maintain a business-like front, and where the absorption of two young people who were in love was going to throw her right into Philip's arms. She had not only let down the bridge, but she had handed him the key to the front door.

The trouble with Philip was that his very quietness led you to underestimate him, she thought grimly, as she jumped out of bed.

She saw no more of him until he called in at the

shop one Saturday evening a week or two later, when she greeted him with a somewhat belligerent gleam in her eye. It was just on closing time, and she was packing a black taffeta frock into a box for a customer. Philip wandered through to the back of the shop, and studied an evening gown with grave interest. A young girl emerged from the door marked "Private," and dashed by him, pulling on her gloves.

"Good evening, Mr. Dallas. Good night, Miss Vale."

"Good night, Hilda. There you are, madam. I think that will travel all right."

"Thank you. I'm very much obliged for all the trouble you've taken. Good night."

"Good night."

Laurian pulled down the blind and bolted the door behind her. Then she began to put the covers over the dress racks.

"Your young Hilda's in a hurry to-night."

"Yes. She's off to the pictures. What brings you, Philip? Or have I forgotten a date?"

"Dear me! That sounds a little frosty. I met your father yesterday, and he said they were expecting you to-night. I happened to be due at Larksmere this week-end, so thought I'd look in and see if you would like a lift."

"Oh. Well, that's very good of you," said Laurian, reflecting that he was an adept at taking the wind out of one's sails.

"Not at all. Sheer self-indulgence, in fact. Shall we have a bite at the Crown before we go?"

And there she was again, cornered neatly with no way of getting out. She frowned at herself in the mirror as she pulled on her hat. She was losing her grip.

Over dinner, Philip submitted their holiday plans for her approval.

"Sölden's a nice little village tucked away in the valley, and there's grand walking as well as climbing. It's years since I was there, but I don't expect it's changed. I hope you'll like it."

"I'm sure I shall. Austria is a new country to me, though I know Switzerland pretty well, and I expect

the Austrian Alps are not very different from the Swiss
Alps."

"No. A little kinder, I think. This will be the first
holiday you've had since going to the shop, won't it?"

"Yes."

"You work too hard, my dear. It's time you eased
up."

Laurian regarded him pensively.

"I wonder just what you mean by easing up?"

The corner of his mouth twitched and there was a
twinkle in his eyes as he said smoothly:

"I think you know. Why have you been avoiding me
these past months?"

"As a tactician, you're pretty good. I've been very
busy, Mr. Dallas."

"What are you afraid of, Laurian?"

He was suddenly serious, and she could not fob him
off when he spoke like that.

"Of losing my little island of independence."

"It's served its purpose. It's helped you to get your
wind back."

"But I want to stay there, Philip. I don't want ever
again to depend on people for my happiness. I want a
free life, uncluttered by emotional ties."

"Well, we usually get what we want, if we want it
badly enough," observed Philip as the coffee arrived.

Which remark, thought Laurian, got her nowhere.
But he turned the conversation to the safe topic of
Continental food, and remained cheerfully impersonal
during the drive to Larksmere until he drew up outside
her home.

"Thank you, Philip. Will you come in?"

"No thanks, my dear. I must be off. By the way, did
I tell you that Julian's wife is expecting a baby in
November?"

"No. So you'll be a genuine uncle soon, then."

"Afraid so. Makes me feel quite old. Pity the
Guv'nor died too soon to see his grandchild."

"Do you like living in a London flat after Bryony
House, Philip?"

"Well, it has its points. Convenient and all that. But

I'm shockingly old-fashioned, really. I prefer a house and a garden. I was damned glad, though, when old Julian took him a wife and I became superfluous. She's a nice girl, and we Dallases need a feminine influx. I began to think that two crusty old bachelors would be the sole remnants of the Dallas family, and that seemed a bit bleak."

"At thirty-four, you've written yourself off rather young, surely?"

"Well, you're the best judge of that. You see, I'm very obstinate. If I can't have the right person, I don't want anybody at all."

"Are you sure that I'm the right person?"

"Absolutely. I always have been."

"But I'm not the same person that I was when you first knew me, Philip."

"Fundamentally, I think you are. You've been badly hurt, you've grown a certain armour, and you're very cautious about giving your heart as a hostage to fortune again. I don't blame you. But it doesn't alter my feelings about you."

"There's an awful single-mindedness about you that frightens me, Philip."

"Nonsense. You're not easily frightened, and certainly not by me."

But she was, she thought, as she slid out of the car and said good night.

It was, therefore, with mixed feelings of pleasure and apprehension that Laurian joined the party which set out for Dover early one misty September morning.

It was impossible, however, to be in the company of Jill and Derek for long without being infected by their gaiety. It was a quality which had been absent from her life for too long, and a good deal of her old vitality leaped up to meet theirs in those first few days when Philip drove across France, through Switzerland and into Austria. Laurian sat in front with Philip, the map open on her lap, while Derek and Jill in the back registered delight at every unfamiliar sight, from oxen-drawn ploughs, and solitary grandmothers brooding, complete with knitting, over their solitary tethered

cows, to the gendarmes, complete with whirling batons
and revolvers, directing traffic in the middle of the
French cities. The weather was hot, the tree-lined roads
ran straight for miles across France and were blessedly
empty, and when on the second day they came within
sight of the Alps, all the old wonder was there for Laurian, while Jill and Derek were overwhelmed to the
point of temporary speechlessness.

It was not until they arrived at Sölden, and Jill and
Derek set about the serious business of climbing, that
Laurian and Philip were thrown on their own resourc-
es, by which time much of Laurian's apprehension
had vanished, and she felt a sense of well-being and a
determination to enjoy to the full this oasis of happiness which had suddenly sprung up. Philip proved
the easy, charming companion he always was whenever
she could forget the issue of marriage which lay between them, and the days slid by bringing a peace
which covered the old furrows and scars as the snow
covered the scored rock-faces of the mountain peaks.

Lingering on the stone bridge outside the hotel one
morning, waiting for Philip, she wished that the holiday
could go on for ever, that time would stop and leave
her suspended here, in this little village where the sun
shone and the river rushed down icy cold from the
mountains, where the people lived simple lives, and
greeted you with a smiling *"Grüss Gott,"* where there
was no rush and the only noise was the sound of the
river and the chiming of cow bells from the meadows
and mountain slopes. Where you could find yourself,
have time to look in your heart and discover the sources of peace.

She smiled as Philip came up, ramming two bulky
packages into his rucksack. In gray flannels, open shirt
and an old tweed jacket, he too seemed a different person from the quiet, urbane Philip Dallas, publisher.

"All set?" she asked.

"Yes."

"I wonder if Jill and Derek reached the peak this
morning. What time did they say they were leaving the
hut?"

"Oh, about three o'clock this morning. They wanted to see the sun rise from the top."

"That must be a wonderful sight. What a nice couple they are, Philip."

"Yes. I'm glad they were able to have this trip. It'll give them something to remember for the rest of their lives."

"They've such courage. They don't see any snags. I envy them."

"Young Jill's got her head screwed on the right way, for all her airy nonsense. I think she'll tackle the workaday problems of marriage on a few hundred a year with plenty of common sense and vigour. She'll wear the pants in that team, without Derek ever knowing it," added Philip, with a little smile.

They were walking up a winding path through a pine wood, and as the climb was quite steep, they relapsed into silence until they stopped at a rough timber seat on a small plateau to get their breath. Laurian looked down at the village, huddled beside the river far below.

"Only two days before we have to start back, Philip. It's a sad thought."

"You've been happy this trip, haven't you?"

"Yes. Happier than I've been for years. And at peace, too. Being with those two, Jill and Derek, and seeing their happiness, has . . . well, I don't know quite how to put it . . . restored faith, somehow."

But before Philip could reply to this, a young woman wearing a gaily embroidered blouse, a red skirt and climbing boots came up to the seat. She was followed by an elderly man with a sporting Tyrolean hat, corduroy shorts and the familiar wide leather braces. With a *"Grüss Gott,"* they sat down, panting. Recognising that mark of the Englishman, gray flannels, the man addressed Philip in halting English, and they were soon all talking about the best walks in the district in a mixture of English and German which was remarkably successful. Philip's German was good and Laurian's sketchy, while the girl's English was non-existent and that of her father erratic and picturesque. It was a bright interlude, and when Philip and Laurian pressed on, their Austrian friends said good-bye as though they had known them all their lives.

After studying the map again, they turned off the main track along a footpath which crossed the face of the mountain, and began to look for a suitable spot for lunch. The path wound through a rich assortment of low berried shrubs and heather. Laurian recognised whortle-berries, dwarf cotoneaster and creeping juniper bushes, but there were many she didn't know. Leaves were reddening on some of the bushes, and with the black, red, purple and blue-grey berries which were so abundant, the carpet was richly coloured. But bushes, as Philip pointed out, were singularly ill-adapted to support human frames in any sort of comfort, and they had to scramble down off the path before they could find a small patch of grass, strewn with boulders, on which they could take their ease.

They accounted for their luncheon packages, large though they were, without any difficulty at all, and Laurian lay back on the grass afterwards with a sigh of utter contentment.

" 'If it were now to die, 'twere now to be most happy,' " she quoted, as she closed her eyes against the sun.

Philip sat smoking, gazing at the mountain peaks on the far side of the valley. She half opened her eyes and watched him idly. The sun had tanned him, and his profile stood out sharply against the pale blue sky: black hair, highish forehead, black eyebrows and lashes, a long, bony nose, a mouth which was firm and didn't give much away, a clear-cut jaw line. What, she wondered, gave him that quiet assurance which she had always found so comforting? Was it born of a mind that knew what it wanted and was never side-tracked? After all, if you knew what you wanted, it saved an enormous amount of wear and tear. No running round in circles trying to decide just what was the good life for your own particular, complicated ego. Or was it born of a sound sense of values, which went a long way to ward off sickening disillusionments? Or did it arise from a life that had gone according to plan? No, it couldn't be that entirely, because from one aspect, it had not gone according to plan at all.

He turned and looked down at her quickly, as though he had sensed her scrutiny.

"Penny for them."

"I was examining your profile and pondering on what lay behind it," she replied, smiling up at him.

"Dear me. That's a little disconcerting. To save you any further efforts at psycho-analysis, I'll tell you that just now, there is only one thought in my head, and that is, how to persuade you to marry me. You've been so happy this week, that I thought the time might be more auspicious than it has been on other occasions."

"Oh, Philip, dear. . . . What can I say? You've been such a very good friend to me, and I'm truly fond of you. But marriage needs more than I have to offer, and you deserve more than that."

"What better basis for marriage than a genuine friendship which has stood the test of time?"

"But why not just friendship, in that case? It's so much safer."

"Because I love you, and I want to live my life with you beside me."

"But I'm not in love with you, Philip. I must be honest about it. I like you immensely. In fact, it's warmer than that—a sincere affection and a great respect. But . . . I've been in love, Philip, and this isn't it."

"It may be the best part," he went on quietly, although she knew by the sudden tensing of his hand that she had hurt him. "What you experienced before may have been exciting, passionate, and powerful enough at the time to sweep you off your feet. Would it have had the staying power that the affection between us has had and will have?"

"I don't know, Philip."

"Love's a word that covers a multitude of feelings, Laurian, but the purely physical aspect can never maintain that high pitch through marriage. It can't. Familiarity alone would make it impossible. It can only change into something more tempered, more lasting, more suitable for daily life together. The excitement goes, and, if it's the real thing, understanding and affection remain and deepen. We have all that matters between us, dear. The fact that your knees don't turn to jelly when I come into the room can't really count against the broad truth that we could live so happily together."

"It's not only that. I've been hurt, and I've hurt other people because of it. I just don't want to get involved again. I should hate to hurt you, and I don't particularly want to bark my own shins any more."

"You can only avoid that by going into a convent," said Philip drily. "I know you're set on being a bachelor girl with a career. All very fine. But is a bachelor woman going to be so jolly? Doesn't that future look a bit barren? I'm not presumptuous enough to maintain that I can give you Utopia, but at least our marriage would give you the warmth and help that close companionship can provide, and it seems to me a better proposition to go through life with somebody's love behind you than to tackle it alone."

"Philip—about the knees turning to jelly. Are you in love with me that way? I mean, do you . . . ?"

"Do I want you in that earthy sense? My dear girl, of course I do. But I still maintain that that is not the most important aspect, and if you can deal with me kindly in that way, I shall be the happiest man alive to have you for my wife. You don't, by any chance, find me personally revolting? That, I admit, would be a snag of the first order."

"No. Far from it."

He shot a glance at her flushed face.

"You know, you might surprise yourself."

"I think I might."

His hand came down on hers.

"Laurian, dearest, I love you with all my heart, and I'll do everything in my power to make you happy if you'll marry me. Will you?"

Her eyes searched his face gravely. He could give her devotion, he could give her, perhaps, some of his own peace of mind. And perhaps she could learn to give him the love which he surely deserved after these years of patient kindness and unselfishness. She prayed so, as she said simply:

"Yes, Philip, I will."

As he stooped to kiss her, she thought, this is the first time any man has kissed me since Roy. . . . And then she forgot about Roy.

Chapter Eleven

THE SUN WAS sinking when they climbed back on to the path, and as Laurian looked back across the valley, the mountain peaks were turning gold. They had to go in single file along the track at that place, and Laurian, with her eyes on Philip's back, thought, after all this time, he's won. And now, I feel that I'm at rest. Dear Philip . . . She stumbled over a boulder and called her attention back to the path.

Two small boys with baskets of cones on their backs scrambled past them. Their mouths were stained with whortleberry juice and they grinned as they sang out "*Grüss Gott.*" They were both fair, with blue eyes, and their bare legs were as brown as the cones they carried.

The path came out to the river, which rushed steeply down to the village, and as they turned round by the church and came in sight of the hotel, they saw Jill and Derek approaching from the opposite direction.

"Here's love's young dream, looking somewhat battered," observed Philip cheerfully.

Derek was a little ahead, carrying a coil of rope round his shoulders, an ice-axe and two rucksacks, while Jill limped along behind, looking all in. They raised a smile when they saw Philip and Laurian, however.

"Good climbing?" asked Philip.

"Wonderful," said Derek.

"Super," said Jill.

Their boots were covered with dust. Derek had a jagged tear in his breeches, his face was peculiarly blotched, the effect of sun and sweat, and he was loaded like a mule. Jill's face was caked in some greasy substance to ward off the scorching effect of sun on the heights, and her eyes looked sore. One of her hands was badly grazed, her white shirt showed stains of perspiration, and she was lurching along as though every step needed a monumental effort. Her cardigan was tied round her waist by the sleeves, and her handkerchief trailed out of the pocket of her breeches.

No, thought Laurian, looking at them; little snags like making the money go round and coping with housekeeping were hardly likely to bother them.

They appeared in good shape for dinner, all signs of battle erased except for Jill's grazed hand, and recounted their exploits with gusto, until Jill broke off in the middle of explaining to Laurian how one ascended a chimney, with:

"I say, do I see champagne?"

"You do, my child," replied Philip. "This is an occasion. You have a peak, and we have an engagement to celebrate."

"I say! Really? You and Laurian?"

"Why not? You haven't a monopoly where engagements are concerned, you know."

And after toasts had been drunk, and a good deal of chaff had been meted out by Jill and Derek, the former observed, with a twinkle in her eyes:

"No wonder you've been such an accommodating chaperon, Uncle Phil. Wait until I tell Grandma."

"Well, for lord's sake don't tell her you spent a night in a hut together. The fact that a bunch of climbers and guides shared it with you wouldn't soothe her sense of decorum."

Jill, who was beginning to feel the effect of the champagne, giggled, and Derek eyed her with mock severity.

"Well, anything less conducive to an atmosphere of illicit love than climbing kit, I can't imagine," said Laurian.

"Ah, but there's romance in a coil of rope and an ice-axe to the initiates," countered Derek.

"Well, we'll make do with the lower slopes, and leave the heights to you."

"Dear Uncle Phil. So sweet of you to fix such a lovely holiday for us. Dear Uncle Phil . . ."

"Heavens, the girl's drooling!" said Derek.

Jill wrinkled up her nose at him.

"No. Just tired and happy."

"Bless you, my children, it's been a very good trip all round. You may not know it, but I owe you two a lot. You'd better toddle up to bed, Jill. You can't go to sleep under the table. It lets the side down."

And after that, the airborne feeling induced by the champagne seemed to remain with Laurian for the rest of the holiday, and when she finally arrived back at Mrs. Marrowbed's house and opened the door of her bed-sitting-room, she felt as though she had returned from a Never-Never Land which she had dreamed.

To bring the reality of it home to her, however, Philip conducted her to a jeweller's on the following Wednesday afternoon, where he spent an hour choosing her ring, and drove her down to Larksmere at the week-end to break the news to her family.

"This is going to give Dad wonderful opportunities for a come-back," said Laurian as soon as Philip's attention was reasonably freed by emergence from the congestion of Richmond. "He backed you very strongly from the first."

"Quite right, too. Have you told him yet?"

"No. I'm going to spring it on him and watch his face. Philip . . ."

"Yes?"

"Would you mind if I keep my interest in Frensham's? I wouldn't give all my time to it, as I do now, but I would like to remain a partner and keep an eye on it."

"Your baby?"

"Yes, in a way. I've had such a fight to buy myself in, and I'd like to go on nursing it and see what I can make of it. I'll have to find a reliable assistant, of course. That is, if you won't object."

"Of course not. I've a perfectly good housekeeper at

the flat who'll stay with me, I'm pretty sure, and take the household worries off your shoulders. And that brings me to my big news. A chap 'phoned me yesterday morning about a house for sale at Kew, and I think it might be what we want. Would you like to run over and see it to-morrow? It's quite small, and the price is steep, but there's a decent bit of ground."

"It sounds just the answer. When is it vacant?"

"Within a month of the sale."

"Oh."

"Did you want a long engagement?"

"No-o. But I haven't had time to realise we're engaged yet."

"You will, this week-end," said Philip, half smiling.

"Too true. I have to break the news to my family to-night, present myself to your brother and his wife to-morrow morning, and choose a house to-morrow afternoon. You're some hustler, Philip."

"We've wasted too much time, my dear."

When he drew up outside her home, he laid a hand on her arm as she was about to get out.

"Laurian, you're not afraid, are you? About our marriage, I mean."

"No, dear, I'm not afraid. I lost my doubts in a Tyrolean valley, which was a nicer end for them than they deserved." She kissed him swiftly. "Come along and help me face the music."

She found her mother and father with Penny in the sitting-room.

"Hullo, folk. I've brought Philip in with me. You're going to see quite a bit of him in the future because we're going to be married."

Her mother paused from her embroidery, and with a calm smile, said:

"Darling, I'm so glad."

Penny merely beamed, while her father put down his book, and, looking at them both over his glasses, said grimly:

"And about time too."

Philip grinned at Laurian's faintly injured expres-

sion. Her bombshell had made about as fierce an effect
as a leaf falling from a tree.

Laurian and Philip were married at Larksmere
Church on a still, sunny day at the end of October.

Penny, fussing round the bride as she dressed for the
event, found her very calm and composed. She wore a
cream brocade dress with a heart-shaped neck, a tightly
fitting bodice and a full skirt which gleamed richly with
every movement. Her face was pale and her brown
eyes looked darker than usual.

"Aye, it's a lovely dress," said Penny. "A dress with
dignity. And you look lovely in it. Let me fix that
veil."

Laurian smiled at her mother as she came into the
room.

"Hullo, Mummy. You look very ravishing. Are you
going to eclipse the bride?"

"Hardly." Mrs. Vale looked at her daughter, and
nodded her head slowly. "Philip will be proud of you."

"It's a proud and happy day for all of us," said
Penny, looking as though she would burst into tears at
any moment.

"Just give an eye to things downstairs, Penny, will
you?" asked Mrs. Vale hastily. "I think everything's
under control, but you might check the seating arrangements. I had so many interruptions, I've probably put
all the wrong members of the families together."

"Poor Mummy! I wanted a quiet wedding, you
know," said Laurian as Penny went out.

"Yes, but think how your father's pride would have
suffered!" said Mrs. Vale, with a smile.

"Quite. Well, I can trust you not to go all emotional
on me."

"Yes, dear. You're looking rather pale. Feel nervous?"

"Not a bit."

Mrs. Vale, watching her, half wished that her daughter was a little less calm. The old, shining vitality which
Laurian had once possessed had never come back since
that affair with Roy Brenver. Now she had poise and

charm, and Philip had brought the warmth back to her smile, but the dancing flame of 'life which had been hers was gone.

"Darling, you are happy about everything, aren't you? You're sure that Philip is right for you?"

Laurian picked up her bouquet of pink and cream roses.

"I suppose nobody can be sure of anything in this life, Mummy, but I believe Philip and I will be very happy together, and I know that it will be my fault if we are not."

Her mother kissed her, and stood back for a final survey.

"Lovely. But I'm still not convinced that my idea of red roses wasn't best. A rich material demands rich colours."

"I didn't want red roses," said Laurian. "Run along, or you'll make me late. Tell Dad I'll be down in five minutes."

When she was alone, Laurian stared at herself in the glass as though she saw a stranger there. In one hour's time, she would be Mrs. Philip Dallas, and the whole course of her life would be changed. There were no hitches this time. The bridegroom had suitable means, the parents approved and the bride was willing. The bride . . . She was back in a hideous sitting-room, with artificial sweet-peas on the table, remembering the wild ecstasy which had swept through her in a man's arms. . . . For one brief moment, she felt a panic-stricken desire to run away. Then she pulled herself back to reality. No phoney sweet-peas, no red roses for defeat. The road ahead had good foundations, and integrity of mind was a better bet than the waywardness of the blood any day of the week.

She stopped at the top of the stairs to lift her skirt, and saw her father pacing up and down in the hall below. He turned as she came slowly down. For once he was speechless, and she could see that he was deeply moved. She smiled as she took his arm. After all, she thought, it was his day, perhaps, even more than hers.

As winter was at the gates, they had chosen to spend their honeymoon at Torquay, from where they returned to the little white house in Kew which Laurian had loved at first sight. If anything surprised her about those first few months of married life, it was the ease with which she slid into it. She had expected a difficult period of adjustment while she and Philip learned the by no means easy art of living in double harness after a free and solitary existence in which they had had nobody but themselves to please. In fact, she found Philip, with his equable temperament and intelligent mind, just as comforting and agreeable in the rôle of husband as of friend, thus confounding the odd moments of uncertainty before her marriage when she had reminded herself that the friend of leisure hours could suffer a sad sea change in the challenging waters of matrimony.

If she had any complaint at all, it was that Philip spoiled her. His anxiety to justify his contention that their marriage would be a success led him to study her too much and himself too little. She was no more adverse to this state of affairs than any normal human being, but she was aware of a queer little ache in her heart at Philip's diffident, faintly apologetic air when he made love to her. It was as though he said, I know this is a bore for you and I've no right to ask it, but if you could just put up with me ... And she felt guilty of a monumental selfishness that this should be so, because she knew that she herself had planted the root of his diffidence when she had made it clear that she was not in love with him. She had wanted to be completely honest, but often in those first months she found herself regretting that honesty. He gave her so much and asked so little.

She tried to voice something of this in the first hour of the New Year. They had been to a ball, and were sharing a pot of tea in front of the sitting-room fire, which Mrs. Brewer had thoughtfully banked up before she went to bed and which now glowed cheerfully in its decline. Laurian was sitting on the sheepskin hearth-rug, with the green chiffon skirt of her dress spread all around her.

Philip, leaning back in his armchair, cup in hand, eyed her approvingly. Even now, there were odd moments when he found it hard to realise that he had really won her after that long drawn-out struggle. Had he wiped out all her doubts? Because, for all the seeming completeness of her capitulation in Austria, she had still reserved a thin line of defense. Her wish to keep on with Frensham's had been more of an instinctive clinging to something in her life which was not dependent on human relations, something she could fall back on if things went wrong, than a love of the job itself. Of that, he was sure. And he knew that her desire to put off the question of children for the time being sprang from uncertainty, from the feeling that they ought to see how things worked out first. And how far had he gone to dispelling those doubts? A little way, at least, he thought. He must have patience, not rush her, in his efforts to restore the confidence which had been so badly shattered in that love-affair. The firelight drew flashes from the emeralds at her throat and burnished the copper tints in her hair. It would be death to lose her now.

The object of his thoughts stopped looking at the pictures in the fire and said:

"Will you make a New Year resolution for me, Philip?"

"That sounds ominous. Are you about to disclose something revolting about my habits that you can't bear any longer?"

"No. I want you to stop spoiling me."

"Great Scott! That's the last thing I expected to hear. I don't spoil you, anyway. But why?"

"Because spoiled people soon begin to take an awful lot for granted, and because you're not being fair to yourself."

"My dear girl, I've never been so happy in my life as I've been these past months."

"You're evading the issue."

"Did you think that up for yourself, or did the idea come from something your father said?"

"I thought it up for myself. Why? Has Dad said anything to you? Come on, out with it."

"Well, he did offer me a piece of advice at Christmas which rather surprised me. Now, let me see, what were his words?"

"Go on. Knowing Dad, I'm sure they were few and to the point."

"As far as I can remember, he said: 'Philip, my boy, don't make the mistake of thinking that all blood is as sensitive as yours. The Vale blood has a tough element in it and a hot-house is the wrong treatment for hardy plants. Bear it in mind.'"

"The old fox," said Laurian, smiling. "He always sees more than you think he does. Now he's robbed me of all that feeling of nobility I had at making the same confession. When somebody else points it out for you, you merely feel aggrieved. But, seriously, Philip, he's right. You mustn't be so self-sacrificing; you must stake your own claims. Otherwise you'll deserve what you get."

"And what do you suppose that will be?" he asked with a swift smile.

"A wife who accepts all her husband's devotion as casually as a cup of tea, which I pray I may never do. But it could be."

"I'm not worried. I have my methods, my love, and I never rush my fences. Your father gets results by different methods, but I usually get what I want in the end, you know."

Laurian shook her head.

"Well, you have been warned. It was a good dance to-night, wasn't it?"

"Yes. Not much in my line, but I must confess that having the best dancer in the room for my partner helped a lot. Do you miss your classes?"

"No. I can always go along and give Uncle Adrian a hand at the Club if I want to. But I've other interests now, Mr. Dallas, and my successor there is very good, even if I did teach her myself."

"That's all right, then. Do you know you look very lovely in that dress. What do you call the material?"

"Chiffon."

"I like it. Soft and cloudy and delightfully feminine. Wasn't that a hideous striped affair of Isobel's?"

"M'm. A little bizarre, perhaps, but then that's Isobel's line."

"Well, I thought it was ghastly. Like a gummy wasp."

Laurian chuckled, thinking that the dress in question had been displayed more for Philip's benefit than anybody's, perhaps.

"How long has Isobel been with your firm, Philip?"

"Oh, ages. About ten years, I suppose. Julian introduced her. She's a distant relative of some kind, all very involved. Her father was a writer, and she's got ink in her blood. She's very clever. On the light side, she's the best reader we've got. She has an uncanny flair for spotting new talent and seldom backs a loser."

"Very useful."

Philip shot a glance at her.

"You don't like her, do you?"

She smiled at him.

"When she comes here, she goes out of her way to talk shop and show up my literary ignorance. Very good for me to be shown what an inadequate wife I am for a publisher, but it tends to make me feel very much *de trop*. In literary circles, I should think she's a raving success."

"She saves me a lot of tiresome entertaining. But I know what you mean. No other world but the writing world exists for Isobel. Personally, I'm only too glad to get away from it when I leave the office, so for heaven's sake don't you go springing any literary aspirations on me. One in the family is quite enough."

"I know my limitations. What talents I have don't lie in that direction."

"Nothing so static as print for you. But your movements are poetry. Did you know that?"

He stood up and held out his hands. As she came into his arms, she wondered if he knew that Isobel

Darney was in love with him. She looked up into his
thin face, with its dark, intelligent eyes, and knew that
those eyes didn't miss much. He would be too much of
a gentleman ever to mention it, though, she thought
with a swift little smile, for Philip's correctness often
presented a tempting target to the mischievous Vale
imp which sat on her shoulder. Her husband raised his
eyebrows in question at her smile, but she shook her
head and kissed him, and he didn't pursue it.

Chapter Twelve

ONE MORNING ABOUT a week later, Laurian walked
briskly along towards Philip's office. She had come to
London to do some shopping, and Philip was taking
her to lunch. It was a grey day, with a biting east wind,
and she was glad to reach the shelter of the narrow
grey building which housed her husband's firm. Philip
was alone when she was shown into his office. He
pushed a manuscript aside and took off the heavy
horn-rimmed glasses he wore for reading.

"My dear, you're frozen," he observed, as he kissed
her.

"M'm. It's lovely and warm in here, though. What a
nice room this is. It suits you, Philip," she added, as
she looked round.

"Does it? You don't think I'd go with chromium,
strip lighting and a battery of telephones?"

Laurian shook her head, smiling. The room, with its
fawn carpet, dark furniture and subdued lighting, was
saved from too sombre a note by the bright bindings of
the books which lined one wall, and the warmth of the
red and gold curtains. Nothing showy, no unnecessary
trifles, no hint of the rushed business man's base. It
might have been a country house library. Peaceful,
comfortable, in good taste. And somehow, in a chaotic
world, enormously reassuring, like her husband.

Just then, Isobel came in with a flurry, and the
peace was disturbed.

"So sorry to interrupt. Oh hullo, Laurian. Just wanted you to have my report on the Bridget Newlyn manuscript, Philip. I think she may be a find."

"Thanks, Isobel. I'll have a look at it after lunch."

"What brings you to town, Laurian? A show?" asked Isobel.

"No. Just shopping."

"Oh, by the way, we have a mutual friend," said Isobel.

Laurian, who was looking at the book-shelves, didn't turn as she said casually:

"Who is that?"

"Roy Brenver. I only found out a few days ago that he was an old friend of yours."

Laurian was still staring at the books and hadn't moved a muscle, but Philip, watching her, noticed the unnatural rigidity of her back. Isobel's eyes were on her, too. Then she turned and said lightly:

"Oh, Roy Brenver. Yes. I knew him some years ago. He worked in my father's firm."

And then Philip rang for his secretary and gave her some instructions, Isobel took her leave, and Laurian went on with her scrutiny of the books. Neither Philip nor Laurian made any reference to Roy Brenver when they went to lunch.

After she had finished her shopping that afternoon, Laurian went to Richmond and called in at the shop to leave some trimmings that were wanted in the workroom, then returned home in comfortable time to bath and dress before dinner.

Lying in the bath, she allowed her thoughts to return to Roy, who had been floating about in the background in a most tiresome manner ever since Isobel's mention of his name. How did she feel about that name now? It could mean nothing to her. She had not thought about him for months, or perhaps it was years now. He belonged to a past which was dead. Yet she could not deny that his name, coming out of the blue like that, had hit her like a sledge-hammer. Silly. He was nothing to her. She despised him, if she felt any feeling for him at all. Yet, in her heart, there was a little seed of fear.

She would hate to see him again. And when her mind demanded the reason, since he was now no longer of any account in her life, she knew that it was because she was afraid, not of the reactions of her mind and her heart, but of the betrayal of her blood.

Then she dismissed these foolish thoughts. She was being extremely childish to harbour them, she decided, as she towelled herself with a vigour that expressed her exasperation with herself. Here she was, married, most happily married, to a fine man, beside whom Roy Brenver was not worth one second's thought.

She decided to put on the black velvet dress which Philip liked, and took particular pains with her toilet that night. When Philip arrived home, he found his wife waiting for him by the fire, his sherry already poured out and a warm smile lighting her face as she turned to him.

"Will I do?" asked Laurian, turning as Philip came in from his dressing-room.

"Let me look. M'm. Definitely." His eye ran over the slim line of the black dinner-gown his wife was wearing. It was beautifully cut, its plainness relieved by gold embroidery at the neck and wrists and on the wide belt which emphasised the slenderness of her waist. "Rather more sophisticated than your usual, but I like it."

"I thought I'd better do you credit in the eyes of your firm, and assume a dignity if I have it not. Do you want me to tie that?"

"Please." He squinted at her as her deft fingers performed miracles with his tie. "Julian's lost his voice, so I have to make a speech. A pity. He's better at putting over the one big, happy family touch than I am."

"You'll perform more gracefully, though. I always have admired that beautiful quiet ease of yours. Do you ever get flustered or furious, Philip? I haven't seen any signs yet."

"You'd be surprised at the storms that rage unseen," he said, smiling.

"Well, if they're raging, let me know about them. I'd

rather share, even if the rest of the world must be kept in ignorance."

He kissed her hair, but he didn't take her up, merely observing:

"Can't say I like office functions, but we only have the one dinner a year, so I suppose I must do my duty with a good grace."

In the dining-room of the hotel which had been chosen for the occasion, little groups were standing about, drinks in hand, while the waiters added the final touches to the long table. Laurian and Philip were talking to Julian and his wife and Mr. Paston, the firm's secretary. Over Cynthia's shoulder, Laurian saw Isobel come into the room with a slight, fair-haired man. For a second, the glass of sherry in her hand trembled and her face stiffened. Philip saw her expression and his eyes followed hers. Then she was talking gaily to Mr. Paston about gardening, which was his passion, and if she looked a little flushed and talked more quickly than usual, only Philip noticed it.

In a few minutes Isobel came up and introduced her companion, and Laurian found herself face to face with Roy for the first time since that day in her father's office more than three years ago. She had collected herself in the few minutes' breathing space which had elapsed since Isobel's entry, however, and she appeared quite composed as she acknowledged Roy, for all the sickening fear in her heart. At a first glance, he hadn't changed at all. The same lively blue eyes, the same air of vitality, the same ready charm. He greeted her warmly, as an old friend, and for a moment the sheer effrontery of it took her breath away. Then, aware of Isobel's appraising eyes, Laurian withdrew the hand which Roy had clasped, saying with a calmness which she was far from feeling:

"Yes, it is a long time, isn't it?"

Philip inclined his head at the introduction, and took Laurian's arm as the waiter announced that all was ready. He could feel her trembling as he led her to the table, and he squeezed her arm. Isobel and Roy were fortunately placed sufficiently far down the table to make conversation with them impossible, and Laurian gave her attention to the hoarse Julian on one side of her and Philip on the other. She liked Julian. He was more stolid, more portentous than his brother, but beneath his stolidity Laurian had found a genuine kindness and consideration, and the same strong sense of duty and responsibility which lay behind his brother's quieter demeanour. Of the two, Laurian knew that it was the quieter man who was the more effective, however. In Cynthia, too, Laurian had found a friend. She was a cheerful, practical young woman, who had two months ago produced a son with the minimum of fuss, and who appeared to manage husband, son and Bryony House with great efficiency and unruffled good humour.

"Everything under control, dear?" asked Philip softly a few minutes later.

Laurian smiled at him.

"Everything under control."

"Good."

The dinner pursued its course, and Laurian, deliberately keeping her eyes from straying down the table, gave every appearance of enjoying herself. In fact, she felt as though she was walking on a tight rope. Philip's speech was delivered as successfully as she had predicted, and she felt proud of him as he stood there, commanding attention quite effortlessly while he thanked the staff for their loyal co-operation, welcomed all guests, added a touch of humour to the sincerity of his praise and sat down to considerable applause.

"Philip does this sort of thing very well," whispered Julian. "Keeps to the point. I always ramble."

"You're very brave to be here at all," said Laurian, restraining the desire to whisper back. "You ought to be in bed."

"That's what Cynthia says. Always have been bothered with my tubes. Confounded nuisance. Can't say the boy takes after me, though. Kicked up the devil of a row last night. Cynthia takes no notice. Amazin' girl."

The amazing girl firmly steered her husband home after the dinner, however, and Philip led off the dancing with Laurian. They were surrounded with people most of the evening, and it was not until the last dance but one that Isobel and Roy broke into their circle, and Roy asked Laurian to dance. In the circumstances, it was difficult to refuse, and she walked silently on to the floor with him. She knew that Isobel and Philip were both watching them. Roy's arm went round her, his hand clasped hers. Now that she was close to him, she could see that he had become a little more fleshy. He was still very good-looking, but there were lines round his eyes, and the faint blurring of his features added a sensuality which had not been there before. His hands were soft and well-kept, and he was faultlessly tailored. He had apparently found his way to the easy life which had been his goal.

"Funny, meeting again like this," he said.

"Not really. You knew from Isobel that I had married Philip Dallas, and you must have expected that I should attend his firm's dinner."

"I did. That's why I suggested I should come as Isobel's guest."

"Why?"

"Curiosity. Wanted to see if you were as attractive as ever. I was also curious to see your husband."

"I can assure you that neither my husband nor I feel the least bit curious about you."

"Come, now. You're not harbouring any ill-feeling, are you? We were kids then. That's all over and done with."

"Precisely."

"You know, you're even more attractive than you were. You've changed. You've more . . . poise; not so eager and ingenuous. I'm almost in awe of you."

"I find you very offensive. Only a person of incredible vanity and ill-breeding would have the impudence to force a meeting in the circumstances."

"My, my! We never used to ride such a high horse. Surely, because an engagement is broken, the girl doesn't have to be uncivil to her ex-fiancé when she meets him?"

Laurian stared at him.

"You really are incredible, aren't you?"

He grinned.

"Don't believe in taking life too solemnly, my dear. Seriously, though, Laurian, there's no reason why we shouldn't be friends. I always liked you . . . a lot. Still do. And you don't dislike me, not in your heart. I know your pride must have taken a knock, but there's no room for pride in this kind of world. What do you say?"

"I'm not in the least interested."

"I see. Quite a girl, Isobel, isn't she?"

"I don't like talking when I'm dancing. Do you mind? And I don't think I'll dance the encore. I'm a little tired."

"Good. We'll sit out and then we can talk. What will you drink?"

"Nothing, thank you."

"Gin and orange, if I remember rightly."

Before she could see anybody to rescue her, Roy was back again with the drinks. Laurian couldn't spot Philip or Isobel at first, then she saw them dancing together on the far side of the floor.

"Have you known Isobel for long?" she asked with deadly politeness.

"About six months or so. She's a friend of a friend of my wife's, if you get me."

"Oh."

"Still not interested?"

"Still not interested."

"Liar. But I'll be kind and tell you. I married a year ago."

"Congratulations."

"Thanks. We've a flat in town, and a house in Kent not far from Isobel. And so you were a good little girl, after all, and married the man of your father's choice."

"I married the man of my own choice. Will you excuse me?"

And Laurian, her face white with anger, crossed the

room to join Philip and Isobel, who had just stopped dancing.

"Philip's dancing has improved a lot, Laurian," said Isobel brightly. "Have you been giving him lessons?"

"No. But he's naturally an easy dancer. Well balanced. If he cared to, he could be tip-top."

"But he doesn't care to? That's a pity, Philip, with such a lovely dancer for a wife."

"I agree. But we've even pleasanter ways of spending our time together," said Philip with a little smile. "Shall we have the last waltz, my dear?"

And, the reassuring comfort of Philip's arms, Laurian's anger subsided and she felt safely at peace again. Here, she thought, was where she belonged. Here she was at rest.

Philip said little as they drove home, and Laurian wondered whether to leave it to him to bring up the subject of the encounter with Roy. It had been a forbidden subject between them always. Laurian had avoided it at first because it was so painful, and then because it was something which she wished to forget, something quite apart from Philip. She had never told him just what had happened to cause the break between them. He had only known as much as her father had told him. And Philip had avoided the subject because he was too well mannered to intrude on such private ground unless he was invited, and because he, too, wanted it forgotten. Now she found it difficult to break their rule. But they couldn't just ignore Roy's presence there that night. This was Philip's first encounter with the man he knew she had once passionately loved. Something would have to be said if the meeting was not to be given a significance which it did not warrant. It was Philip, in the end, who brought it into the daylight, just as she herself was seeking an opening while she brushed her hair in front of the dressing-table mirror. He spoke carefully, as though feeling for every word.

"I'm sorry Isobel brought that chap along. She couldn't have known, of course, that he was the last person you would want to met."

"Couldn't she?" asked Laurian drily.

"Oh, no, my dear. Isobel wouldn't do a tactless thing like that. She doesn't know that you and Brenver were ever engaged, I'm sure."

"Roy is not the person to keep such things to himself, Philip. Isobel knew all right."

"I think you're mistaken."

They had certainly got off on the wrong foot, thought Laurian, as she said lightly:

"Well, let's not argue about it. It doesn't matter. That old business is over and done with now. What did you think of him, dear?"

"Brenver? He was younger than I expected. I didn't like the impudent way he looked you over. In fact, I'd have liked to punch his head for his blasted cheek."

"And so would I."

"It upset you, didn't it?"

"It was a shock, at first. But if you mean it made me unhappy seeing him—it didn't. It only made me ... angry. You don't have to worry, Philip," she added, half laughing to stave off any embarrassment which her too sensitive husband might feel at her frankness.

Phillip was moving rather restlessly round the room.

"Isobel told me that he is married to the widow of John Russet."

"Who was he?"

"A stockbroker. Pretty big man in his line, too."

"How fortunate for Roy," observed Laurian. "Stop prowling, darling, and come to bed. Your speech was a gem to-night. Do you know something?"

As he came up behind her, she caught his hands and imprisoned them on her shoulders, tilting her head back to look up at him.

"I felt immensely proud of my husband to-night."

"My dear ... I ..." He stumbled helplessly, then took her in his arms. "I love you so much, Laurian."

"I know, darling."

Two mornings later, Laurian received a letter. She recognised the spidery writing on the envelope as soon as she saw it on the breakfast table. She would have preferred to postpone reading it until she was alone, but that would look rather pointed. She frowned as she tore it open. Philip was glancing at *The Times*.

DEAR LAURIAN,

I'm sorry if I seemed impudent the other night. I didn't mean to be, but I guess it was the result of the kick I got out of seeing you again. Will you forgive me, and be friends?

I know I let you down, and I don't pretend to any great virtue, but don't forget that I knew what it was to be poor, and you didn't. Anyway, can't we remember the good times we had together, and forget the rest? After all, things haven't turned out badly for either of us, I guess, so what's the point of bearing any grudge?

ROY.

Laurian put the letter back in the envelope as Mrs. Brewer brought in the coffee. She intended to tear it up, but wondered whether to show it to Philip first. Her instinct was always to be open about everything, but she was beginning to feel that it was possible to be too candid. The love which she had once felt for Roy, and which she had foolishly brought again to Philip's notice when he asked her to marry him, was, she knew, a very painful point in Philip's consciousness, so that now she felt that she had to walk warily to save rubbing it. Their rôles seemed to have changed. It was Philip who was now so sensitive about Roy. It would, perhaps, be wiser to ignore the letter altogether. . . .

She tore it up and threw it in the waste-paper basket. It was of no importance.

"I've a rotten throat this morning," said Philip. "Think I'm hatching a cold."

Laurian lingered outside the florist's shop on the way home that afternoon. It was nearly dark, and the day had been wet and cold, so that the spring flowers in the brilliantly lighted window had more than a touch of magic about them. There were great bowls of daffodils, tulips, white lilac and mimosa, behind rows of potted hyacinths and cyclamen. It was impossible not to feel a lift of the heart at such a lovely blaze of colour. The rain spattered down again and she dived into the shop and bought some tulips and daffodils. It was pouring as she came out, and a man was sheltering in the doorway.

"Hullo. I thought that was you I saw window-gazing."

"Roy! What are you doing here?"

"Coming to call on you, as a matter of fact."

"Why?"

"To see if you'd accepted my apology. You got my letter?"

"Yes. I'm still not interested, so you needn't bother to call."

"Well, let me give you a lift home then. You'll get drenched in this, and the flowers won't be improved."

Laurian hesitated. It was coming down in buckets, and the Jaguar car parked at the kerb was very handy. The wind whipped off a man's hat in front of them and sent it spinning down the road.

"Come on; don't be a Muggins. You'll never be able to keep that umbrella up in this gale, and it can't hurt you to drive in my car for five little minutes."

"Righto. Thanks."

"Let's run for it."

He took her elbow and they dashed across the pavement to the car. In the car, Roy seemed in no hurry to start.

"You're a sight for sore eyes with those flowers."

"Thank you," said Laurian lightly.

"Look here, you're not really still angry with me, are you? You can't be after all these years."

Laurian looked at him steadily. All at once, she was seeing him in a new light. It was as though the mists of the past had cleared away, revealing the man as he was now. She had been blinded by passions before: by the passion of first love and by the passion of bitterness at its betrayal. Now, with her mind unclouded by emotion, she saw him objectively for the first time. Like all parasites, she thought calmly, he was greedy. He had chosen his path, and he had followed it successfully. He had gained what he was after, but he still wanted more. He wanted the best of both worlds. Or perhaps, she thought, now that he had achieved his ambition, it seemed a little sterile. Every line of his handsome face seemed to spell out to her a self-indulgence that was almost pathological. And in that moment of silence, she knew that she was free, and her heart sang a song of triumph. At last the past was truly buried, or not so much buried, she thought, as withered away.

"How vain you are, Roy. I'm not still angry with you. You just don't matter any more. Can we go now?"

"I'm not swallowing that. Your face gave you away when you first saw me the other night. What's the objection to our being friends? Is your husband the old-fashioned, possessive type who doesn't believe in his wife having men friends? He looks as though he might be."

"I am not discussing my husband with you. Or anything else. I assure you that whatever I may have felt for you in the past, you leave me quite cold now. If you're not going to start, I'll walk."

Roy started the car with a jerk and nothing more was said until he drew up outside her house.

"Good-bye, Roy. Thanks for the lift. And I mean good-bye."

"So long," he rejoined, unabashed, and drove off as Laurian dashed across the pavement to the shelter of the porch. As she let herself into the hall, she felt a rush of happiness sweep over her. Here was home and Philip, here was her peace, her harbour. The last chains of the past had fallen from her, and she felt as light as air. From the kitchen came the sound of a Beethoven symphony. Mrs. Brewer had a taste for the classics on the radio. Laurian began to sing with the orchestra the last movement of the Pastoral symphony as the front door opened and Philip came in. She turned, the flowers still in her arms.

"Hullo, darling. You're early."

"Yes. I knocked off. Felt too muzzy to cope with any more work to-day."

"Dear, you're soaking! Couldn't you get a taxi from the station?"

"None in sight. They're nice."

"Yes. I couldn't resist them. I didn't see you, but I've only just this minute come in. I bumped into Roy Brenver outside the florist's and accepted a lift to save being drowned."

"Yes. I saw him drive off. I'd better change."

Laurian watched him walking upstairs. He looked tired out, she thought, as she took the flowers out to the kitchen. It was a pity he had to be reminded of Roy again.

After dinner, Philip settled down to read a manuscript he had brought home, but he gave it up after half an hour.

"You'd much better go to bed with a hot drink and a couple of aspirins, dear," observed Laurian.

"Yes, I suppose so."

"I'll bring you up hot whisky and milk—Dad's sworn remedy for everything."

"Righto. I'll sleep in my dressing-room, Laurian. No sense in passing a cold on to you if we can avoid it."

"Oh, I'm not very susceptible. I shouldn't worry about that."

But he insisted, and Laurian went off to see about hot bottles. Her husband, she deduced, like most healthy men, took minor ailments hardly. As she was accustomed to her father's preoccupation with the respective merits of cremation and burial as soon as he had a cold, she ascribed Philip's silent withdrawal in the days that followed to a similar depression, and did her best to make a fuss of him and cheer him up. But although the cold ran its course and departed, Philip remained detached and distant, and the old, easy intimacy between them seemed to have evaporated.

Chapter Thirteen

AT THE END of January, the south-west wind which had brought so much rain changed to the north, the thermometer dropped with a bump, and after a week of hard freezing the snow came.

Laurian never forgot that spell of severe weather. It seemed to her afterwards that the real trouble between her and Philip took shape for the first time on the day the snow arrived, although she had been troubled by an uneasy sense of something seriously amiss for the past week or two. It was not that Philip was any less pleasant and considerate than always, but she felt that he had withdrawn from her, that he was standing apart, troubled with something that he was hiding from her. She could not believe that a man as intelligent and mature as Philip could be jealous of Roy now, when there was no cause, but somehow the resurrected Roy had cast a shadow between them, and she didn't know how to dispel it.

The day started badly, for Laurian had a headache and Philip overslept. As she poured out coffee, the first flakes of snow were drifting past the window.

"I don't think I'll go to the shop to-day. I've rather a lot to do here," she observed. "Oh, I forget to tell you, Philip. I 'phoned Jill yesterday to see if she and Derek would come to dinner to-night as well. I knew you wouldn't mind."

"Of course not. They're not exactly Isobel's type, though."

"No. They're mine. I like them, and three's an awkward number. Jill and Derek will be able to keep me company while you and Isobel talk shop."

"Just as you please, of course."

And why Isobel had to come to dinner at all, thought Laurian crossly, she didn't know. The woman saw plenty of Philip during office hours. The fact that she was in some remote way connected with the Dallas

family, and that she always had new discoveries in the
literary world to discuss with Philip and apparently in-
sufficient time to do so at the office, seemed to Laurian
inadequate reasons for social obligations. But then, she
thought, sighing, Isobel obviously thought the world of
Philip, and no man could be expected to be so devoid
of vanity that such admiration didn't evoke a certain
friendly response.

The day passed quickly in shopping and helping
Mrs. Brewer to prepare for the small gathering that
evening. As she put the finishing touches to the table,
Laurian surveyed the pretty little dining-room with
pleasure. The snowy scene outside the window emphasised the brightness and warmth of the room with
its log fire, soft green carpet and trios of gold lights on
the walls. The daffodils in the centre of the table were
like a pool of sunshine, and the glasses round them
glistened as brightly as morning dew.

Isobel arrived first with Philip. She came in laughing,
shaking the snow from her fur coat.

"Hope you don't mind, but I found your umbrella
most useful," she said, as Laurian welcomed her. "Roy
asked me to return it to you. You left it at his place the
other day."

Laurian stared at the umbrella Isobel was holding
out.

"What place?" she asked coolly.

"His flat."

"I've never been to Roy's flat. I've no idea where it
is. I left the umbrella in his car the other day when he
gave me a lift in the rain. As a matter of fact, I'd quite
forgotten it."

"Oh well, I daresay I misunderstood him. Anyway,
here it is, with many thanks for its existence. It saved
my hat from a snowy death."

"Come up and take your coat off, Isobel, and then
have a drink. I'm sure you need one to warm you."

Philip took the dripping umbrella from Laurian and
went out to the kitchen with it. When Laurian and
Isobel came into the dining-room, he was attending to
the drinks.

"Sherry for you, Isobel?"

"Please."

"Laurian?"

"The same, please."

Laurian looked at Isobel as she stood by the fire, glass in hand. She was a tall, slender woman, with good features and shining black hair worn close to her head. She had a musical voice and a charming smile. She wore a black and white dress which fitted her like a sheath. Laurian disliked her with all the lusty vigour of her Vale blood. That there had been malice behind Isobel's explanation about the umbrella, Laurian did not doubt. She turned with relief as she heard Jill's high-pitched voice in the hall. It would be like a breath of fresh air to see those children again.

With the help of Jill and Derek the evening passed off pleasantly enough. At first, the two young people seemed to find Isobel a little awe-inspiring, but this soon wore off, and before the evening was over, Jill was telling Isobel all about their economy drive with a view to marriage before the next winter.

"We can't stick another winter apart," said Jill ingenuously. "The summer's not so bad, because we can get out in the country and be alone, but wet, cold fields are no good to anybody, and Granny never goes out."

"Excuse my fiancée," said Derek, grinning. "She's an outspoken girl. Don't ask me to have a cigarette," he said, waving his hand as Philip pushed the box over. "That's one of the economies, and the one that hurts most. If I start again, I'm lost."

"Don't you dare," said Jill. "If I can make do with a bun for lunch and darned stockings and positively no clothes, you can do without cigarettes. Do you know any way of raising money, Laurian?"

"Well," said Laurian, smiling, "when I was in dire need, I took dancing classes. What about that?"

"Hopeless. I'm a rotten dancer."

"You've said it, girlie," said Derek.

"Now don't start again," retorted Jill, laughing at him. "We had an awful row about that a few days ago," she added to Laurian. "At least, it started with that and sort of led on to other things. You know how it is."

"It's all ended amicably, apparently," said Philip.

"Oh yes. We enjoy making it up so much that it's almost worth having a row for," said Jill.

Which was all very well when you were as young as Derek and Jill, thought Laurian. But somehow, when you were older, it wasn't so simple as that.

"Does she get violent, Derek?" asked Philip.

"Often. But she's such a little scrap of a thing, that I have no difficulty in coping."

"That's the stuff."

Jill grimaced at them, then sighed happily.

"That was a wonderful dinner, Laurian. You've no idea how beautiful luxury is when you're in the throes of economising. Buns every day are awfully jading to the palate."

And so they went on, chattering happily, while Isobel dethroned for once from her rôle of leading conversationalist, eyed Jill and Derek with a faint air of incredulity mingled with amusement. Laurian had seen the same expression on the faces of people at the zoo watching the monkeys.

Philip drove their guests to the station that night, and while she was waiting for him by the fire, Laurian decided that she must have this absurd business of Roy cleared up. She could not insult Philip by accusing him of unfounded jealousy, but this skating round the subject for fear of hurting each other was getting them nowhere. She would explain to him how she had felt when she first saw Roy, and just how she had discovered that he meant nothing in her life now. Philip would recognise and understand the truth when he heard it. She had been foolish to avoid the subject just because it was so sensitive. And at first she had been afraid that, against all her reason, her senses might still have fallen a victim to Roy's charm. Now that she was certain of herself, she must somehow convey that certainty to Philip.

But this admirable plan was scuppered by the first

quarrel which she and Philip had ever had, and which flared up as soon as he came back.

"Hullo. Was the road bad?" she asked.

"No. Not too bad." He came across to the fire and stood with his back to it. "Well, that's that. A very pleasant evening. By the way, we're not doing anything at the week-end, are we?"

"No. Why?"

"I've promised Isobel we'll go to her place. If this weather holds, we'll get some skating down there."

"Oh no, Philip, not a whole week-end."

"Why not? Julian and Cynthia will be going, and you like skating, don't you? There's a grand stretch of water near Isobel's house."

"But can she put us all up? What about food?"

"She can manage. Or, at least, her housekeeper can. She's just received a food parcel from friends in South Africa, and the neighbouring farmer knows her pretty well and can oblige with poultry."

"I'd rather not go, Philip."

"Well, I'm sorry, my dear, but I'm afraid I've promised for both of us. After all, Isobel accepts our hospitality, and I suppose she likes to return it. We went skating there two years ago. That was when Isobel's mother was alive. Julian was very much attached to the old lady. We had a most enjoyable time and Isobel thought it would be fun to repeat it now that the weather's suitable."

"That may be, but I think you might have consulted me before committing me to a week-end party."

"I naturally thought you'd be pleased at the prospect."

"Did you?"

"Yes. I know you don't much like Isobel, but Julian and Cynthia will be there, too, and Isobel's presence surely won't affect the enjoyment of the skating?"

"I prefer not to accept the hospitality of people I don't like."

"If you entertain people, you must expect to be entertained by them some time or another."

As Laurian looked at the tall figure of her husband

standing in front of the fire, his face serious but quite calm and self-possessed, she felt her temper rising. He had shut her out of his confidence, treated her with polite consideration in all inessentials and as though she were a stranger in all essentials, and now he was forcing her into the company of a woman she distrusted and disliked at a time when she needed to give all her attention to solving the problem of their own troubles, troubles which were of his making.

"I'm sorry, Philip, but I won't go. You must make some excuse for me and go yourself if you're so keen."

"I don't like telling lies or offering snubs to my friends."

"Then you shouldn't have treated me like a piece of luggage," she flashed.

"Why don't you like Isobel?"

"For many reasons. One being that she detests me, another that she's malicious, and another that she's a liar. I can go on if you wish."

"That's quite enough, I think," said Philip coldly. "Have you any real grounds for those accusations?"

"Yes. The lie she told about my umbrella to-night was deliberate enough."

"She admitted that she might have misunderstood Brenver."

"She doesn't misunderstand anything."

"My dear, I've known Isobel Darney, and her family, for years. You've met her not more than half a dozen times. Don't you think you might be mistaken?"

"No."

"You've not always been a good judge of character, you know."

Laurian flushed.

"Perhaps not. I'm better when it comes to my own sex, though."

"You don't think my judgment, after years of knowing and working with Isobel, is likely to be sounder than yours?"

"In this case, no."

"You have a poor opinion of my insight, apparently."

"No. In some circumstances, a man's vanity is apt to provide blinkers," said Laurian drily, and had the satisfaction of seeing this go right home. The scores were even.

"And a woman's possessiveness?" suggested Philip. Laurian went white with anger.

"You mean, I'm possessive about you?"

"Oh no. I wasn't thinking of myself."

"Who, then? Please explain, Philip."

"I wondered whether you resented Isobel's friendship with Brenver."

For a moment, Laurian felt sick. She had not, even in her most worried moments, imagined that the gulf between them had grown so wide.

"How dare you say that, Philip," she said softly.

He looked at her gravely.

"I didn't say that it was so. I said that I wondered if that might be behind your unreasonable hostility to Isobel."

"How dare you even wonder it."

"Is it true? Does it contain, at least, a bit of the truth?"

"It doesn't contain a shred of truth. It's a complete and abominable lie."

"Then I apologise, Laurian."

"Thank you."

That was the worst of Philip, she thought. You could never shake his self-control. Always he had himself in hand. Always. He was like rock, and she wanted to blast it.

"Well, we still haven't settled the question of this week-end," he said. "I didn't realise that your dislike of Isobel was so strong. Naturally, I shan't expect you to entertain her or be entertained by her again now that I know, but I must ask you to make an effort to put up with this week-end, now that I've accepted."

"That sounds like an order, Philip."

"It's a request."

"A distinction without a difference in this case, I think."

Her eyes met his, but he was not to be moved. He

was quite relentlessly imposing his will on hers. She looked down at her hands, then stood up and walked across to the door. She turned as she opened it.

"Very well, Philip. I'll go with you at the weekend. If you wish to entertain Isobel here, I shall, of course, play my part. But on no account will I ever again accept an invitation of Isobel's. Good night."

As she walked slowly upstairs, she wondered how it was that in such a short time they could have come to this state of affairs. She had welcomed in the new year with such happiness and confidence in her marriage, and now, with only five weeks of the year gone, it seemed to have crumbled round them.

Alone in the bedroom, she paced up and down, going over the scene angrily and unhappily. She feared no interruption. Philip had kept to his dressing-room ever since his cold gave him the excuse, and her pride had been too hurt to query his preference. It was some time before she heard him come upstairs, and for a long while after that, she tossed and turned in bed. It wasn't fair, she thought. She had made one bad blunder with Roy and she had paid for it. Now she was being made to pay all over again. And Philip, who throughout all those years had never failed in kindness and understanding, now seemed a stranger.

Jealousy, a poet had written, was as cruel as the grave. But that Philip, so sane and well balanced, should fall a victim to it on such flimsy evidence seemed incredible. And why wouldn't he discuss it with her if it troubled him? Or was he ashamed to admit it, as he should be. And to accuse her of jealousy on account of Isobel's friendship with Roy—that was the last straw.

And round and round went her thoughts, tormenting her, driving away sleep.

The remainder of that long week was painful in the extreme. Laurian, angry and hurt, remained on her dignity, and Philip accepted her attitude with a politeness which was very studied. No further reference was made to the week-end visit until Thursday night, when Philip raised the subject.

"It's a nuisance, but I've got to have dinner with one of our authors to-morrow night. He's over from America and sails back on Saturday, so there's no help for it. I think you'd better go down by the four o'clock train, as I can't be sure which train I shall catch, though it's bound to be pretty late. Probably the ten-five."

"You're not driving down?"

"No. Isobel says the road's blocked at Westerham Hill, and conditions are pretty bad on all of the Kent roads, according to the A.A. Isobel's place is twenty minutes' walk from the station, but she says she'll arrange for a car to pick you up, and I can walk it if need be."

"How and when is Julian going?"

"He and Cynthia went down by train with Isobel to-night. Julian's in a flap in case a thaw sets in, so he's given himself and Isobel a day's holiday from the office, and they're starting operations to-morrow. Julian's a very fine skater, you know. Won quite a few trophies in his time."

"I didn't know. He looks rather heavily built for that kind of sport."

"M'm. He's put it on lately, of course."

"Can't I wait and go down with you to-morrow night?"

"Better not. I don't want to have to watch the clock, and it would mean keeping you hanging around indefinitely. I think you'd better stick to the train I originally intended to catch, and I'll follow when I can. Leave your case for me to bring."

"Very well. I'd better go and pack it now."

All arrangements had been made with Isobel, thought Laurian angrily as she put her suitcase on the bed. It only remained for the rebellious child to do as she was told. She hated everything about this week-end. It was being pushed down her throat like a dose of nasty medicine, and it was going to take all her will-power to swallow it. She was not good at playing a part, at hiding her feelings. And nothing would horrify her husband more than a display of naked feelings in the company of Isobel and his brother.

When she had finished packing, she slipped downstairs for a hot drink before going to bed. Now that she and Philip were living like strangers in the same house, she saw no necessity to do more than call out good night as she passed the sitting-room door, but it was ajar as she went by and, glancing in, the words froze on her lips. Philip had evidently not heard her steps on the carpeted floor outside. He was still sitting in the armchair where she had left him, but he was leaning forward with his head in his hands in an attitude of despair that went to her heart. She wanted then to run to him, to fold him in her arms and comfort him. But as the impulse came to her, he looked up and saw her, and the mask dropped.

"Hullo, my dear. Finished packing?"

"Yes. Philip . . . you look so tired."

"I've a bit of a headache."

You've more than a headache, my dear, she thought, as she said:

"Can't I do anything?"

But he ignored the appeal in her eyes and smiled briefly as he replied:

"No, Laurian, thanks. I'll take some aspirins and turn in." He went to the window and drew the curtain back. "It's snowing again. You'd better wear good strong boots to-morrow in case Isobel can't get a car to the station."

"Good night," said Laurian, in a voice as cold as the snow outside.

Chapter Fourteen

THE TRAIN HAD stopped in a cutting. On the slope, every twig of the thicket of bushes and trees carried a crest of snow on its upper surface and showed black on the under-side, so that the whole presented a lovely, delicate study in black and white, like an old print. At the foot of the slope, the snow was unbroken, and the only birds to be seen were two black-birds fluttering among the trees, so that the colour scheme remained intact. The beauty of it caught at Laurian's heart as she looked out from the corner seat of the carriage. She felt sorry when the train moved on with a jerk, carrying her nearer to her destination. She dreaded the moment when she would have to greet Isobel with a smile, and pretend that all was well. Perhaps Julian would be there to meet her instead. She hoped so. But it was neither Julian nor Isobel who awaited her at the little station, but Roy in his Jaguar.

"Hullo, Laurian. Nice to see you."

"What are you doing here?"

"Playing errand boy for Isobel. Hop in."

"But I didn't know you were included in the party."

"If you don't mind, we can talk more comfortably in the car than in this blizzard. God, what weather!"

Laurian turned to him as he handed her a rug for her legs.

"Are you staying at Isobel's, too?"

"No. Only joining you for dinner to-night. Isobel sent out an SOS to me this morning for some logs. She's almost out of coal and the coal merchant can't promise any because the road up from the railway siding is blocked with snow and his men are down with 'flu. I filled the back of the car, hence its dirty condition, and trundled them down."

"I see. And now?"

"Now the girl's been let down by the local wine merchant, so I'm off to raid my wine cellar. She asked me if I'd mind picking you up on the way. All clear?"

"More or less. Do you live near Isobel?"

"Five miles. Only ten minutes in the car normally, but it took me nearly half an hour this morning. The roads are pretty bad round here."

"Are you going to fetch the wine first, before dropping me?"

"If you don't mind. There's a nasty little hill between here and Isobel's which is very icy, and I'd rather not tackle it more often than I need. My place is the other side of the station. Isobel didn't think you'd mind the detour in the circumstances."

"It means unpleasant driving for you. Is the wine so important?"

"The whole week-end will be wrecked for Isobel if there's no wine to offer her guests," said Roy, grinning. "To ask the Dallases to dine without wine would, I gather, be as bad as asking them to sleep on the floor."

"I think that's putting it rather strongly," said Laurian as he cautiously let in the clutch.

"Well, there it is. Anyway, it's no trouble. The poor girl was in an awful stew this morning. Everything that could go wrong had, including the freezing of the bathroom pipes. A foot or so of snow in a place like this seems to disorganise the whole works. One thing, we shan't meet much on the road."

It was dark by now, and, once clear of the village High Street, they seemed to be isolated in a muffled, dead world. The headlights showed deep ruts in the snow, and the car sent up showers as it went. The ruts were icy, and Laurian felt the car skid once or twice.

"It's worse to-night than it was earlier," observed Roy. "It was beginning to thaw this morning, but it's freezing hard enough now."

"Don't you think you'd better turn back, Roy?"

"Windy?"

"No. But you don't want to get the car stuck for the night."

"True. We're nearer my place than Isobel's now, though. Easy does it."

He handled the car well, and Laurian had driven too much herself to be nervous, but she thought they were attaching absurd importance to a few bottles of wine.

They met nothing else on the road. She kept quiet, knowing that Roy needed all his attention for the road. When they turned off the main road into a narrow lane which rose fairly steeply, with banks of snow each side, he said cheerfully:

"Good. I'll be all right now. No ruts. There's our place just off on the right."

"You're very isolated. Is it a farm you have then, Roy?"

"M'm. Fruit farm. Smallish. Oh, damn, that's torn it."

Across the road ahead of them lay an elm tree, brought down by the snow. Roy drew up.

"Is there any other way round?" asked Laurian.

"Yes. But only by a road that I know was blocked this morning. The lane's too narrow to turn in, anyway, and I don't fancy reversing down that hill. Looks as though we'll have to walk it. We're not far. Only about ten minutes. Got boots on?"

"Yes."

There was nothing else for it. To try to reverse down that narrow, twisting, slippery hill in the dark was crazy. The car would never hold the road in those conditions.

Roy covered the radiator with two travelling rugs and helped Laurian out.

"Give me your arm. It's deep here."

The snow came well over her boots, and it was heavy going.

"We're in a jam, Roy. What are we going to do? How can I get to Isobel's?"

"Short of a helicopter, my dear, you can't. You'll have to stay here for the night. It may be better in the morning. If I can't back the car down the hill in daylight, we can probably get something out from the village to pick you up, but nobody will budge to-night with roads like this. I didn't realise they were so bad."

"Well, I hope your wife won't mind having me dumped on her."

"She won't. She's in Madeira at the moment. This is quite an adventure, Laurian. I'm beginning to enjoy myself."

"Are you?"

"M'm. Rather cursed myself for my altruism in acting as Isobel's messenger boy to-day, but I'm beginning to think that virtue is rewarded, though I've never entertained the thought before."

Laurian said nothing, but thought a lot. Here was a pretty kettle of fish, indeed. The week-end with Isobel which Philip had forced on her looked like turning out to be a week-end with Roy. Poetic justice for Philip, perhaps, but it was going to put her in an exceedingly awkward position in more ways than one. As they walked up the drive to the long, low building which was in darkness, Laurian said:

"Who is looking after you, Roy?"

"The foreman's wife. They live in the lodge over there on the far side of the orchard. Come along in. Welcome to my domain, Laurian," he added, grinning wickedly as he switched on the hall light.

"You're enjoying this, aren't you?"

"Enormously. For once the gods have planted a real plum in my lap. I've wanted a session alone with you ever since I saw you at that dinner."

"I suppose it is the gods, and not your engineering?"

"The gods, my dear, though I couldn't have done it better. As a matter of fact, I didn't know your husband wouldn't be with you until Isobel mentioned it at the last minute."

"And then you decided that you must collect the wine before you dropped me?"

"That was agreed to mutually by Isobel and myself. But I didn't fell the elm tree, and it wasn't down when I left this morning. Come on. Relax and enjoy yourself. When a situation arises that is inevitable, make the best of it. The Chinese have a better way of putting that, but it might embarrass you. Afraid we'll have to look after ourselves. I sent Mrs. Lyon off when I thought I was dining out. She's got a rotten cold, and I can't very well ask her to plough up here to-night. Do you mind foraging? Let me take your coat. Feet wet?"

"Yes. The snow came over the top."

"Give your boots to me. I'll find you some slippers. The radiators are warm, but we'll want a fire. Perhaps you'd light it. Matches on the mantelpiece. I'll be with you in a minute."

She lit the fire, feeling rather helpless and not knowing quite what to do about it. Then she tidied her hair and looked round her. The room was large and beautifully furnished. On the bookcase was the photograph of a woman with a smiling face. Laurian walked across

for a closer inspection. It was the head and shoulders
of a stoutish person who had once been pretty, and
who now, in middle age, retained traces of a baby-
faced prettiness which seemed a little pathetic. The
kind of looks that made it difficult to grow old with
dignity, thought Laurian.

"My wife," said Roy, coming up silently behind her.

"Oh. Why didn't you go to Madeira with her? It
would have been pleasant to escape our winter."

"Yes. But our foreman left just as we'd made arrangements to go, and we thought I'd better stay on a
bit here until I saw how the new man shaped and
whether I could trust him to carry on."

"And can you?"

"Haven't made up my mind yet. Jessie had a bad at-
tack of bronchitis. She's subject to it. That's why I persuaded her to go to Madeira for a few months." He
dropped a hand on her shoulders.

"Know what this is?"

He held up a small twig bearing two leaves.

"No."

"A piece of mistletoe."

"No, Roy."

"Oh yes, Laurian. Just to remind you of the good
times we had."

He kissed her slowly and expertly.

"Unpleasant?" he queried teasingly, as he released
her.

"No. Hadn't you better 'phone Isobel?"

"Yes. I was just going to. Here are some slippers."

"I'll have a word with her when you've finished."

"Righto. There's some sherry in that cupboard. Or
gin if you prefer it. Pour out what you want and give
me a sherry, there's a good girl."

He picked up the receiver, watching Laurian as she
crossed the room.

"That you, Isobel? . . . Yes. Afraid we've got stuck,
my dear . . ."

Laurian poured out two sherries as he explained the
situation.

"I know, ducky, but it can't be helped. . . . I'll look

after her . . . Now then . . . We'll see what it looks like in the morning and 'phone you. . . . Sorry about the wine. . . ." He chuckled at something, then added, "Laurian wants a word with you. Hang on."

Laurian took the receiver, and Isobel immediately rushed into speech.

"My dear, I'm so terribly sorry. I feel it's all my fault, though I did tell Roy not to go any further than the station if the roads were bad. But he's a naughty boy. He and that car of his are part of each other and he won't admit that any conditions are too much for them. Are you all right?"

"Yes, thank you. But . . ."

"Now don't worry. Roy will make you comfortable. I know that. And I'll explain to Philip. Everything, just everything, has gone wrong with this week-end, so it's bound to thaw so that we'll have no skating, and then you'll be able to get back here all right to-morrow."

"Isobel, there's no possible way of getting back to-night that you can suggest, I suppose? Do you think it's any good trying to walk it?"

A small shriek from the end of the line was followed by:

"Darling, no! Out of the question. Philip would never forgive me if I let you run such risks. Don't worry. I'll see that his mind is set at rest about you. It isn't as if I didn't know that you were in good hands."

Philip would appreciate that, thought Laurian grimly.

"Well, if I have any bright ideas, I'll 'phone you again, Isobel."

"Do, my dear. And tell that naughty creature to look after you properly. But I shouldn't call him naughty, because he's been a perfect Samaritan to me to-day, and without his help, we'd all be perishing of cold here at this moment. Bless you both. 'Bye."

"Good-bye," said Laurian.

"Well, there we are, all cosily settled. You and I together here, and Isobel with her pet Dallases there. A very good arrangement, in my opinion."

And in Isobel's no doubt, thought Laurian. With

Philip to pair off with, she would be quite happy.

"By the way, Roy, does Isobel know we were once engaged?"

"Yes. Any reason why she shouldn't?"

"Oh no. I just wondered."

Roy put some more coal on the fire, then poured out two more sherries.

"To the gift from the gods, my dear. They cheated us once before. Now, perhaps, they're making up for it."

"The gods didn't cheat, Roy. You did."

"You know, I rather admired your old man. How is he?"

"Well, thank you. You never admit responsibility for anything, do you?"

"Responsibility is a depressing word, my dear. Like duty. I avoid 'em both like the plague."

"That's obvious. Are you happy now that you've got what you were after? A paid first-class passage through life."

"Very. You've always had that, though, haven't you?"

"No. I left home after our engagement was ended and earned my own living. I had no money then except what I earned."

"What on earth did you do that for?"

"You wouldn't understand. But don't make my ignorance of poverty your excuse any more, Roy. I know now what it is to work hard for a bare living. As a matter of fact, it wasn't nearly as bad as you made out. I rather enjoyed the fight and my independence was worth every bit of it. But independence is something that makes no appeal to you, of course."

This time, she thought, she had made a small dent in his complacency.

"Now look here, my sweet. We're shut up here for the night, for better or worse, and I intend that it shall be for the better. I'm not going to quarrel with you over the past, or about those principles your father was always trotting out. I've sized the world up to the best of my ability, and I play my hand accordingly. If an unexpected ace pops up in it, I'm only too happy to take advantage of it. Now, are you going to be an agreeable companion and forget your sermonising?"

"I'll not lecture you, if that's what you mean. It would be a waste of breath, anyway. We don't talk the same language."

"Signs of sense at last. What's worrying you, Laurian? Something's gnawing at you, besides my sins. You couldn't help this happening, and what does it matter? You merely accept my hospitality for a night instead of Isobel's, in unforeseen circumstances that are beyond question. Don't tell me," he added, his eyes sparkling, "that you're afraid your husband won't be altogether happy about it?"

"I'm the person who is not happy about it."

"So your lord is a jealous lord! Well, well. Must say he gave me the impression of being a bit possessive. Not a type I really care for. Too much of the old aristocratic touch. You know. His foot's on your neck, but it's placed there so charmingly and unobtrusively, that you don't notice it at first. Too bad if he should lose his sleep to-night on your account. Surely he trusts you!"

"I don't think you're being a bit funny."

"No? It's a situation with very humorous angles, in my opinion. Cheer up. There's nothing you can do about it, you know."

"I might think of something if you'd stop talking."

"An excellent reason for chattering on like a monkey. But there is nothing to be done, my dear. You might as well accept it. After all, Isobel will explain. No blame attaches to you at all. By the way, I haven't asked you before, but how do you like being married to Philip? You thought him a stuffed shirt at one time, I remember."

"I always respected him."

"Ah, but respect is a chilly bedfellow, my dear."

"I'm not going to discuss my private affairs with you, Roy. You are of no interest to me now. I despise you. It would be an insult to Philip to discuss him with you."

"Oh lord, we're off on the lecturing again! You may

despise me, and respect Philip, but do you prefer my kisses to his? Come, my dear, in one sense we were always meant for each other, and you know it. All the conventions in the world won't alter that fact, and you're a hypocrite if you deny it."

"It could have been like that," she said slowly. "In fact, when I first saw you again, I was frightened that it would. Women have loved rotters before now, knowing them to be rotters. Reason doesn't always enter into love. But, to my enormous relief, I found it wasn't so. I loved you, heaven knows, in those early days. But I'm not the same person as I was then—nor are you. The years make their mark on us, I guess. What we do becomes part of us, changes us. No action is cut off clean after it's concluded. It's all there, in us. I'm explaining this badly, I'm afraid. You lied and stole from that girl in my father's office, Roy. You lied to me and then sold me out. You no doubt lie to your wife and cheat her, but more cautiously because she's bought you. She owns you. Do you think all that corruption hasn't changed you? Do you think that even you, with all your cynicism and self-assurance, can get away with it without being changed, even from the man I knew, when you were only half-way in, so to speak. Heaven knows, I'm no saint, but with Philip I do stand on sure ground and I wouldn't put a foot on your boggy ground again for anything in the world. When our road divided, it took us a long way apart, Roy. That's the truth."

"I loved you, Laurian, in my way, as I never loved any other woman."

"In your way! You don't really know what love is, Roy. In love, perhaps, but not love. You'll never know what that is, because you love yourself too much to leave room for anybody else."

"Who was going to stop lecturing?"

"I've finished."

"Good. You're growing like your father, you know. You ought to watch it. Now, shall we cry pax and just enjoy this little interlude, as ships that pass in the night, so to speak?"

"Very well," said Laurian lightly.

He crossed the room and turned on the radio. After some fiddling, he found some dance music, and turned to Laurian with a bow.

"Can't dance in slippers on carpet," she said firmly.

"But the hall has an excellent floor, and you could dance on stilts. Come on."

They waltzed round the hall. Roy held her very close, his cheek against hers. In spite of her efforts, she found it a physical impossibility to hold herself stiffly while dancing. He was a clever devil, she thought, as the rhythm caught her up. It was a mistake to agree to this, although the time had to be passed somehow.

"You were mine before you were his," he murmured.

She didn't reply. There seemed nothing to say. His amazing vanity would never allow him to believe that she no longer found him attractive, and she knew quite well that he was confident of breaking down her resistance. He had always been attractive to women, and his success in that field gave him no reason to suppose that he couldn't re-kindle a fire that had once burned so brightly. The vanity and arrogance of the man, she thought. Well, she'd play him at his own game. Nobody was going to treat Laurian Vale as a puppet to be manipulated by strings. Neither Roy Brenver nor Philip Dallas, she decided, suddenly on her mettle.

Roy kissed her ear as she slid out of his arms at the end of the dance and returned to the fire. He followed her.

"No more dancing?"

"No more dancing. And no more to drink unless you can find me some food first," she added, as he went to the sherry. "Your methods are awfully obvious, you know."

He grinned.

"They'll serve. I'll go and scout round the larder. If you want to explore upstairs, it's all yours."

"Thanks. Bathroom?"

"First on the left at the top of the stairs. You'll find a towel in the airing cupboard."

Laurian took plenty of time to wash her hands. She

had to think this situation out carefully. Roy was obviously all set for a pleasant evening of lovemaking. She did not think that he would use force if persuasion failed. Roy was out for a pleasant evening, not a free fight. In his opinion, plenty of drinks, plus his own charms, would make the persuasion irresistible. It seemed, therefore, that she was committed, at least, to an evening of amatory skirmishing. To Philip, already jealous of Roy and the past, this might well be the last straw. The situation between them was now at such a delicate stage, that the knowledge that she had stayed the night with Roy in an empty house might ruin all chances of coming to an understanding. If only she hadn't made Philip believe by those few words that her feeling for him was so pale beside her early love for Roy. Such a few words, and so damaging in their effect. For Philip was neither jealous nor petty by nature, she knew. It was she herself who had sown the doubt.

She pulled her mind back from the past to the present issue. It was Roy, Isobel and the past against her happiness with Philip. Well, she had fought stiff battles before, and this one was more important to her than any. She wasn't going to lose it.

There was a look of her father about her as she stood there, summing up the position, deciding on her plan of campaign.

There was only one thing to do: get back to Isobel's. And the only way to get back to Isobel's was to walk. Roy had said the distance was about five miles, say two hours' normal walking time. That would mean three to four hours in present conditions. She glanced at her watch. Ten minutes past seven. She could get to Isobel's between ten and eleven o'clock if she started soon. She would have to go back down the hill to the main road, and follow that until she reached the station. There she could ask the way.

She drew the curtain and peered out. It was still snowing. The prospect was not exactly pleasant.

"Laurian!"

"Coming."

"You've been a long time." He watched her as she ran down the stairs. "Prettying up?"

"Who for?" she asked, half smiling.

Roy took her arm confidentially and marched her back to the fire. He looked very pleased with himself.

"I've discovered some soup, a tinned ham, cheese and fruit. How about that for our menu?"

"Sounds marvellous. And I'm starving."

"I've a really good hock to go with it, and we might round off with coffee and liqueur. Grand Marnier suit you, or do you prefer Chartreuse?"

"Grand Marnier, please."

"Right. You going to help me assemble the feast?"

She smiled up at him from the depths of the arm-chair.

"Certainly not. You're the host. I'm going to enjoy being waited on by you, Roy Brenver."

"Well, I shall expect to be suitably rewarded. I'll give you a sherry to keep you occupied while you wait."

"No thanks."

"Well, I will, to fortify me before I wrestle with that tin of ham."

He poured it out and sat on the arm of her chair to drink it.

"Remember St. James's Park, and Ma Jenkins?"

"I remember."

"And how easily your skin used to bruise. Such a white skin, I remember. Are your arms still as white, Laurian?"

"I don't see why they should have altered," she said drily.

"Show me. Let me see if Philip leaves his mark. Don't wiggle or I'll spill the sherry. Damnit, I have."

He put his glass down, and unbuttoning the cuff of her dress, rolled up the sleeve. Then he stooped and kissed the inside of her arm, running his lips down to her wrist.

"Just as white, and never a mark."

"Roy, are you going to get me something to eat before I die of starvation or not?"

"I'm a bit peckish myself, I must confess. Think you might come and help me, though."

"I'm much too comfortable."

"Settling down better now, aren't you?"

"Your sherry was good."

"You've no idea how well you become this house. Make the place kind of cosy. All right. I'll go. Give me a kiss first. . . . I said give me a kiss, not take one."

Laurian felt a little shaken when she left her, and there was no doubt at all in her mind about the importance of getting away. She moved quickly. From her bag she fished out her fountain pen and tore a blank page from her diary. After a moment's thought, she scrawled:

"Nothing doing. Am taking a nice, healthy walk back to Isobel's. Good-bye."

She propped this against the clock on the mantelpiece, stuffed two apples into her bag from the dish on the sideboard, and crept out to the hall, hoping that the heating of the soup and the opening of the tin of ham would keep Roy busy in the kitchen for a little while. It was a pity about the soup and the ham, she thought, as she pulled on her boots, slipped into her fur coat, and let herself quietly out of the front door. She left it open, fearing that he might hear if she shut it. There were a few flakes of snow drifting down, and Siberia could not have looked less inviting. Already the footprints they had left an hour earlier were half obliterated.

She pulled her hat down firmly over her ears, and stepped out.

Chapter Fifteen

IT WAS A queer experience, trudging along through the snow in a deserted world. There were no stars, and the sky seemed to press down heavily over the countryside. The snow had drifted in places across the lane, and at one point Laurian found herself pushing through a drift which reached to her knees. By the time she came out to the main road, she was very wet and cold. Here, she thought, it would be easier going, for traffic during the day had carved out ruts which were now only an inch or two deep in snow. But it was, she found, quite difficult to walk in a rut with an icy base beneath the snow, and she slithered and stumbled many times. Her hopes of getting a lift seemed dim, for the road was silent and empty. The only vehicle to pass her in the whole distance between the lane and the station was, in fact, one bicycle which was pushed by a burly man encased in oilskins.

"Nasty night," he observed as he passed her. "Far to go?"

"To the other side of Sandwell station. How far am I now, would you say?"

"About two miles."

He looked at her curiously, hesitated, then, with a muttered good night, he went on a little way and turned off down a side road.

There wasn't much good about it, thought Laurian, as she munched her last apple and put her head down against the icy wind. She was beginning to feel exhausted, and only the doggedness of her determination not to be beaten took her past an isolated farm house which might have sheltered her. Her boots were sodden and as heavy as lead, so that she walked clumsily and jarred herself with a couple of falls. She was pausing for breath after the second of these when she thought she heard a whimper. It seemed to come from the side of the road. She went to investigate, and found only a snow-filled ditch. She was turning away when she heard it again. It came from her right. She moved along to the foot of a tall tree, and stooping down she peered at the humped, snow-covered roots. She made a noise, and was rewarded by a whine, at which she put down her bag and began to excavate. She found him in a hole formed by two gnarled roots bridged by a battered petrol can: a small, round body which she drew out gently.

"Now how on earth did you get there?" asked Laurian.

The puppy, trembling with cold and fright, whined and then licked her chin. He was black, with long ears. A spaniel of about three months, she guessed. There were no houses near, and she could not imagine how he had arrived in that predicament. He had no collar, and was damp and bedraggled.

"Well, I can't leave you here," she said, stroking the small dome with one finger. "You'd better come along to Isobel's too."

She stowed him away inside her coat until only the top of his head was visible, and almost immediately he snuggled down without any fuss and went to sleep.

For some reason, the presence of the pup comforted her. At least, there was one living creature at large with her that night. And on she plodded, feeling that this road had no end.

When, at last, she saw the station in a dip ahead, she stopped to look at her watch. Its luminous hands recorded the unhappy fact that it was twenty-five minutes past eleven. The hope which had urged on her flagging steps for the last mile died. The train which Philip had expected to catch was due ten minutes ago. And as she worked it out, she heard the train come in. Why couldn't it have been twenty minutes late instead of ten, she thought, almost in tears. She was still a good ten minutes' walk away, and Philip wouldn't hang about. To know that he was there, just ahead, and not to be able to reach him seemed the last straw.

She resisted the impulse to sit down and cry. She would never get up again, and a night out in the snow wasn't to be recommended. She lurched along down to the station.

There was no porter to be seen when she arrived there, but she could hear a whistling from the platform at the foot of the stairs. Laurian looked at those stairs stupidly. If she could get down them, she certainly couldn't get up again. Then the porter appeared and came up to the booking office.

"Can you tell me if a tall, dark man came off that train?"

"Yes, miss. The only passenger. Had a couple of suitcases."

"Oh dear." Laurian moistened her lips. "Well, can you direct me to a house called Greenways in Maple Avenue?"

"Sure, miss. You go to the right outside the station, up over the hill, and Maple Avenue is the first on the left going down. It's a bit of a pull, and you look done up."

"Yes. It's not really walking weather. Thank you. I'll make it."

Laurian never knew quite how she managed to get up that hill. A numbness seemed to have descended on her so that she walked as in a dream, and she found herself going blindly past Maple Avenue before she realised she was there. The house was not far along, and as she fumbled at the latch to the gate she swayed and almost fell through, twisting her ankle, although her feet felt so dead that she was not aware of much pain. She hobbled up to the front door and leaned against the bell. She had made it.

Isobel herself opened the door. Laurian blinked. Behind Isobel, she could see Philip at the telephone. He still had his coat on.

"Hullo," said Laurian weakly, and she saw him turn and slam down the receiver. Then he had brushed the astonished Isobel aside, had gathered her up and was carrying her into the sitting-room.

"Sorry to arrive so late, Isobel," she said, "but the walk was longer than I thought."

Then, as the room spun round her and Julian and Isobel and Cynthia seemed to blur and waver as though they were under water, she turned her face into Philip's shoulder, and had no clear idea of what transpired until she found herself in an armchair in front of a bedroom gas-fire with Philip on his knees easing her boots off. She winced.

"I've twisted that ankle a bit," she said.

"Yes. It's swollen. Can you get into a hot bath?"

"Yes, of course. Philip . . ."

He kissed her forehead.

"Never mind now, darling. Explanations will do in the morning. A hot bath and bed for you straight away. What's this?"

He drew out the pup from her coat.

"My mate. I picked him up from a ditch on the way. Give him some milk and a warm bed, dear."

He looked at her with an odd expression on his thin face. But she was desperately tired, and she could only manage a small smile, which was meant to be reassuring, and accept his ministrations.

Dear Philip, she thought, as she lay in bed, blissfully aware of warmth and comfort stealing over her. He had gone to fetch some hot milk for her. She hoped the pup was as comfortably bedded as she was. When Philip came back, she would tell him. . . . But what it was she would tell him, she never worked out, for when he came in she was fast asleep, and he took the milk away.

When she awoke next morning, it was some moments before she could recollect where she was. The bed next to her had been slept in, but was now empty. Outside the window, she could see the snow-laden branches of a fir tree. Snow. She closed her eyes. At that moment she felt that she never wanted to set eyes on snow again. Her body ached and her ankle was stiff. Otherwise, she felt all right and very hungry. She had arrived at this conclusion when Philip looked in.

"Ah, you're awake. How do you feel?"

"Stiff and hungry."

"Reassuring, if not romantic. I'll lay on breakfast."

"What's the time, Philip?"

"Just on eleven."

"Heavens! Don't bother about breakfast. By the time I'm up, it will be lunch."

"Nonsense. You must have something."

"No, I don't want to bother Isobel at this time of the morning. If you could scrounge me up a cup of tea, I'll see about putting in a public appearance. I'm afraid

I'm being a troublesome guest," she added with a little smile. "I haven't held up the skating, have I?"

"No. At least, Julian and Cynthia have gone off. Julian was shocked at the lack of skill displayed by his wife yesterday, and he's going to give her a little instruction."

"Where's Isobel?"

"Messing about in the kitchen, I believe. I'll fetch you some tea and have a cup myself. We're all a bit edgy this morning, I'm afraid."

And what, wondered Laurian, was behind that? Poor Isobel. Having, either by luck or connivance, tucked Laurian securely away with Roy for one night, if not for longer, it was too bad that such an admirable disposition of her guests should have been ruined by one person's obstinate refusal to stay put.

Isobel brought in the tea, followed by Philip.

"My dear, how are you after that terrible ordeal?" she asked dramatically.

"Oh, very well, thank you, and ashamed of having slept so long. It wasn't really terrible, you know. Just rather hard going."

"Well, I still feel it was crazy to attempt it. But then, I'm no walker in the best of weathers. Not the hardy, outdoor type at all. I scolded Roy on the telephone last night for letting you attempt such a journey, but he said you walked out on him when his back was turned and there was nothing he could do about it."

"Quite right," said Laurian cheerfully. "As a matter of fact, Isobel, Roy Brenver isn't really my choice for a week-end companion, and I was so anxious not to be left out of the party here, that the walk was well worth tackling."

She smiled at Isobel, and Philip turned away and studied the scene outside with serious concentration.

"How sweet of you, dear. And how brave. But then, I believe you come of a very . . . tough family."

"Tough as old boots. Roy Brenver has reason to know that. How is the puppy?"

"Oh, adorable!" exclaimed Isobel, glad of the change

of subject. "Creating havoc in the kitchen, but a darling. Whereabouts did you find him?"

"About two miles the other side of Sardwell Station. A little less, perhaps. He was in a ditch underneath the roots of a tree. Can't think how he got there."

"Probably belongs to the Landry kennels. They breed cockers. But they're a half a mile or so back from the road. I'd better telephone and find out. I'll leave you to Philip, dear. So glad you're none the worse for your adventure."

When she had gone, Philip poured out the tea, and sat himself on the end of the bed. He looked at his wife gravely.

"Why did you do it, Laurian?"

Here it came, she thought. The superficialities were over. Trust Philip to go without delay to the heart of the matter. She thought for a moment, trying to put the complexities of the situation into a nutshell. Then she said simply:

"Because I didn't want our marriage to break up. I thought that if I stayed there with Roy, you would never believe that he meant nothing to me. You haven't believed it these past weeks when all you had to go on were insignificant trifles. I was afraid that a compromising situation like last night's would be fatal."

"Was it compromising?"

"I was alone with Roy in his house."

"What about his wife?"

"She is in Madeira. His housekeeper was safely out of the way in the lodge beyond the orchard. Isobel didn't tell you all that last night, I suppose?"

"No. As soon as I heard from her that you were stranded at Brenver's house, I got on the 'phone to you there. All Brenver had time to say was that you'd skipped it. Those were his words. Then you turned up, and I cut him off. Isobel rang up afterwards to tell him you had arrived."

"I guess he wasn't in too sweet a temper. Philip ... you would have minded, wouldn't you?"

He walked to the window and put his cup down.

"Yes. I'm ashamed to say that I should have minded

damnably. But I've been minding damnably for weeks now. I've been in hell."

"You put yourself there, dear. And took me a little way with you. But last night I realised that if I stayed, I should be giving you the last little shove, and I'd have died rather than do that. Philip . . . why have you shut me out? Why haven't you talked to me about it? You haven't given me a chance. I was going to tackle you about it after Isobel came to dinner last week, and then we had that beastly row about this week-end. I don't understand your attitude over this. It's so unlike you."

"I didn't talk to you about it, Laurian, because I knew that you would be honest, and for once in my life, I was afraid of the truth. And I wanted to come to a decision in my own mind before we brought the truth into the open."

"A decision on what?"

"Whether a man who marries a woman knowing that she is not in love with him has the right to keep her to her bargain when she finds she loves someone else. It was a decision I had to make on my own. I knew you well enough to be pretty sure you'd stick to your bargain, even if it meant unhappiness and frustration for you. I had to decide for the two of us. I'd laid seige to you so persistently for so many years that I almost hounded you into marrying me. And even then, you were quite honest about not loving me. Had I the right to hold you in those circumstances? And if I did, could I be happy knowing that you were not? That's what I was trying to decide, Laurian, and believe me, it's not been easy."

"Don't you think you might have found out first if I did love anyone else?"

"I knew you did."

"How?" she asked, astonished.

"Do you remember arriving home in Brenver's car with those flowers that wet evening?"

"Of course."

"Your face when you turned to me told me the truth. I'd never seen you look radiantly happy like that before. I'd never brought that look to your face. And if a few flowers and a lift in the car with him meant all that to you, well . . . I couldn't hope to compete."

"Oh, so that was it. I begin to see glimmerings of daylight. With the past colouring the present for you, I suppose you recalled the jim-jams I exhibited when I first saw Roy again and the note which I tore up—you guessed who that was from, didn't you?"

"Yes."

"I might have known. As I was saying, the jim-jams, the note, the umbrella incident, and my supposed jealousy of Isobel and Roy . . ."

"I did apologise for that."

"Don't interrupt. You added all that up and came to the conclusion that the happiness I'd found with you had been blown away by my revived love for Roy Brenver. Well, it's got a lot of holes in it and it assumes a lot, but I suppose it is just possible. I certainly am glad I didn't stay last night to cap it."

"Laurian, does this all mean that . . .?" He removed her cup, and held her shoulders so tightly that she winced. "You mean, you don't love Brenver, after all? That I've been wrong?"

"Wildly wrong, darling. Do you think that the peace and contentment of mind that I'd found with you, Philip, could be thrown aside so lightly? That all these years of understanding and kindness and devotion that you've given me haven't amounted to something worth far more to me than any brief excitement which Roy Brenver could kindle? You yourself told me how little that one aspect counts in the whole. Why have you gone back on yourself?"

"Because passion is not a rational animal, Laurian. I've lived long enough to learn that. And I knew how deeply you had loved Brenver, and I knew what you went through when you lost him."

"Do you know just how things broke up between us, Philip?"

"No. Your father implied that it was money. I gathered that he refused to back the two of you because he mistrusted Brenver. That's all I ever knew."

"I think I'll tell you all the sordid details. It may help you to understand."

She told him.

"Not a pretty picture, Philip, is it?"

"It certainly isn't," he said grimly.

"When you saw me looking so happy that night, it was because I'd just seen that picture in its true light. In a way, it reminded me of Dorian Gray. All that Roy had done was marked clearly in his face for me that evening. And I knew that I was free of him. It was quite simple and immediate. That was why I felt so happy. Because, at first, I had been a little afraid. And that evening, I knew that there was nothing to be afraid of. And when I got indoors, just before you arrived, I felt that I'd really come home at last, that I belonged there, to you and our home and the children who would come. And I knew that it was the best thing that had ever happened to me."

"Oh, my dear. . . . And then I did my best to wreck it. Can you forgive me?"

"You don't have to ask that. It was partly my fault, anyway. But after seeing you keep such a steady course for so many years, I wasn't prepared for such antics."

"I love you so much, Laurian. The thought of losing you nearly drove me mad. I loved you before I married you, but that was a pale thing beside the love that I have for you now. You've knitted yourself into my heart, into my life. I felt I couldn't go back to the pointless emptiness of those years without you. Not now, not knowing . . ."

"Philip, dear. . . . I have no intention of being un-picked from you, whether it is your hands that try to do it or anybody else's, so you needn't worry. I think later on I'm going to lecture you on one aspect of this business that rather bothers me, but just now, will you kiss me?"

And they were kissing when Isobel knocked and put her head round the door to announce that she had turned on the bath water for Laurian. She went away abruptly, and Laurian's eyes were mischievous as she reached for her dressing-gown. She groaned, however, as she stood up. Every muscle seemed to be protesting. Philip inspected her ankle and insisted on being called to rebandage it after her bath.

"Yes, my lord," she said demurely, hopping along on one foot. Then she added: "You know this week-end's turning out a lot better than I expected."

"Laurian, would you like to keep that puppy?"

She turned, her face eager.

"Could we? I mean, will the owners let us?"

"If the owners are the breeders, as Isobel suggsted, their business is to sell pups, my sweet."

"I'd love to have him. He was a great comfort to me last night, although he was sound asleep all the time."

"I'll 'phone them. If they agree, I'll see if I can get over there this afternoon to pay them and collect his pedigree. He looks a good 'un to me."

"But what about the skating?"

"Oh, the others can go. You're out of it now, anyway."

"Isobel won't like it."

"That won't worry you."

"I'm very un-Christian, aren't I?"

"You're a little wilful sometimes, my love. You finished a few points ahead in that sparring match with Isobel this morning, I thought."

"Can't get a Vale down."

"All the same, you're going to be very nice to Isobel for the rest of this week-end."

"Why?"

"Because, although this morning I'm ready to heap ashes of repentance on my head and go on my knees to you to beg for forgiveness, and although I want to get the sun and the moon and the stars to lay at your feet, in this little side skirmish over Isobel I mean to have my way. No good for you to get away with everything. So are you going to be good?"

"Yes, of course." She blew him a kiss from the door. "Anyway, my father always says that when you're the winner, you can afford to conciliate. *Au revoir.*"

"You Vales!" exclaimed her husband.

Her head came back round the door.

"I say, Philip."

"Yes?"

"Isn't it grand to be talking to each other again? I don't count the sort of polite chilliness which has been passing between us like nasty little snowballs."

"Yes, it's grand. Shall I see if the bath water's overflowing?"

"Oh help! I go. See you later."

When Julian and Cynthia arrived back for lunch, they brought the news that the wind was changing, and might cause a thaw.

"That's the worst of this confounded climate," grumbled Julian. "Nothing consistent about it."

"Are any buses running?" asked Philip. "I want to get to the kennels this afternoon to complete the haggling I started over the telephone just now for this object."

He stirred the object in question with his toe, but the pup had no intention of being deflected from his task of tearing *The Times* into five million shreds.

"But you're going to join the skating party, Philip, aren't you?" broke in Isobel quickly. "It may be our last chance. You won't mind being left, Laurian, will you?"

"Of course not."

"You must come, Philip," went on Isobel. "If the weather holds—and Julian's been predicting a thaw ever since he arrived, and it hasn't come—the village people are going to bring lanterns, and set up a refreshment stall and make a do of it to-night. I thought we'd have a rest after lunch, an early tea, and then go along to the moat in force."

"Think you'd better count me out as Laurian's crocked."

"Oh, but it will all be spoilt if you're not there, Philip. I'm sure Laurian wouldn't want that."

"No. You go, Philip. It may be years before you get a chance to skate again. I shall be quite happy here. Isobel has some opera records I want to hear."

"If I can hire a car, and the road's possible, how

would it be if I drove you over to-night to look on for a bit, my dear?" asked Philip.

And in the end, after a lot of arguments and suggestions through which Philip sailed unperturbed, he had his way. Isobel, obviously intensely disappointed, went off after lunch to rest, leaving Julian dozing in an armchair and Laurian holding wool for Cynthia to wind. Philip spent ten minutes on the telephone trying to hire a car, and eventually succeeded. Then he went off to pick the car up and try out the road to the kennels.

After he had gone, Laurian felt suddenly tired. In bed, the aches hadn't felt so bad, but now that she was up, she had to admit that the bruises from her falls and the hampering effect of her ankle were making life a little uncomfortable, and she longed to be home again now that the unhappiness which had seemed so alien to the little house at Kew had lifted. And she wanted to talk to Philip, alone.

Chapter Sixteen

PHILIP BLOTTED HIS copybook by arriving back late for tea. He apologised, blaming the bad state of the roads and the obscure position of the kennels. Isobel, Julian and Cynthia went on ahead to the moat, and Philip promised to follow with Laurian in due course.

"That was a bleak stretch of road you walked along last night, Laurian. Bad enough in a car," said Philip, as he cut himself a slice of cake.

"Yes. It was the ruts which were so troublesome."

"The snow last night has levelled it again, but it's only half frozen and darned skiddy. A good pedigree, isn't it?"

Laurian looked up from the pedigree which Philip had tossed in her lap on his return.

"Yes. Most impressive. Any explanation as to how the pup strayed that far?"

"M'm. They had a litter indoors because a kennel had been damaged by the snow, and the small boy of the house had broken all rules and taken this particular body out with him in his toboggan. The toboggan came to grief, the small boy damaged his leg and got a black eye, and the pup vanished in the confusion. However, all's well now. I presume you don't intend to call him by that yard-long name given there."

"No. I thought Jet would do."

"Excellently."

He poured himself another cup of tea and brought it over to the couch. Laurian shifted her legs and he sat down on the end.

"You look done up," he observed. "I can't forgive myself for last night."

"It wasn't your fault."

"If I hadn't behaved like a blithering idiot, you woudn't have been driven to it."

"Perhaps not. But I rather think I should."

Philip looked up quickly.

"It was like that, was it?"

"What do you think? A nice little supper, lots to drink and no possible interruptions to mar Roy's technique. It was all so cheap and obvious. The vain little . . . Well, never mind. I wish I could have seen his face when he read my note, though."

"I shall have much pleasure in punching his handsome nose if it ever comes within reach of my arm."

"Don't worry. It won't. I think we'll drop that piece of dirty linen into the fire and forget it now, don't you?"

"Agreed. Give me a kiss. I don't intend to hurry to the party. . . ."

With two rugs round her and a hot-water bottle to hug, Laurian found the car a comfortable base from which to watch the proceedings. The moat, set in a wild stretch of sandy heath about a half a mile from Isobel's house, looked delightful that night with coloured lanterns dotted about and several car headlights trained on the ice. Near Laurian, a man had a brazier and was selling roasted chestnuts, while further round the bank a stall did good trade with cups of tea. And as she watched the skaters glide by with varying skill, she chafed at her enforced idleness, and would have given much to join them. Philip had a few short spells of skating, but he didn't leave the car unattended for long.

Julian, however, had been right about the weather, and soon after eight o'clock a self-elected committee decided that conditions were no longer safe, and the skaters were warned off. The moat was deep, and there had been fatal accidents before. Laurian was not altogether sorry, for she was beginning to get cold, and although she did not want to spoil the fun for the others, it was a little galling to be inactive there in the car.

Back at the house, Isobel suggested a game of bridge before they went to bed. Laurian, as Isobel knew, did not play, so once more she took a back seat on the couch while Philip and Isobel played Julian and Cynthia. But nothing that Isobel could do to make her feel *de trop* mattered to Laurian now. Things were all right between her and Philip, and she didn't grudge Isobel any crumbs of comfort she could pick up.

"Double," said Julian to a call of Isobel's, and Laurian saw Philip's eyebrows go up. It was amusing to watch them. Julian slow and ponderous in his calls, his wife a little hesitant and cautious, Isobel brisk and alert, and Philip urbane and poker-faced. Laurian was watching him when he looked across the room to her and gave her a quick little smile which warmed her heart.

"If you'd led your diamonds earlier, you'd have got home, Isobel," he observed calmly, as he collected the cards.

Isobel looked annoyed, and Laurian smiled to herself. She was learning quite a lot about her husband this week-end.

Few things being more depressing than a thaw, the party broke up early the next day. Cynthia and Julian, wishing to get back in time to see their son before he was asleep, went off by the three o'clock train. Isobel tried to persuade Philip to delay his departure until that night, but he insisted on catching the five-fifteen. He thanked Isobel so charmingly for the week-end, however, that he left her no room for a grievance. Her good-bye to Laurian had a chilly little ring, for all her powers of acting. Her look conveyed that Laurian had really been a great handicap to the party. And so she had, thought Laurian, as she waved good-bye from the hired car.

When Philip opened the front door and she limped over the threshold, she heaved a sigh of relief and contentment.

"Oh, it's good to be home, Philip. It's good to be home."

"You've only been away a couple of days."

"Is that all? It seems ages."

After they had unpacked, they settled themselves in front of the fire for the rest of the evening. With coffee and sandwiches on the little table between them, and two pairs of legs stretched across the hearth-rug, the atmosphere was one of domestic peace. But when they had finished and Philip had removed the table, he sat on the edge of his chair, took out his cigarettes, and said:

"Now, what's bothering you. Shoot."

"I'm not exactly bothered."

"You've been very quiet and thoughtful for the past twenty-four hours, and you've been studying me with a deliberation that's quite unnerving. I have an idea that I've been weighed up and found wanting, in spite of your lenience towards my recent sins. Come on. I'm ready to take it."

"Well, I have made a discovery about you that's a bit alarming, Philip, and I can't think why I never spotted it before. It's alarming because I think it could cause us unhappiness. It's your arrogance that I mean, dear."

Philip couldn't have looked more astonished if she'd accused him of being a thief.

"Arrogant? Me?"

"Yes, you. I've had a lot to think over this weekend, and plenty of time to do it in. It seems to me that all my life I've been up against domineering, arrogant men. First my father, who loved me and thought he should shape my happiness and my life for me; then Roy, who merely used me to further his own ends; and now you. And in a way, you're the most dangerous of the lot because it's so well hidden. I mean, there's no mistaking it in Dad—it sticks out a mile. And Roy's aims are so putrid, that sooner or later you find him out. But something Roy said about you wasn't far off the mark. He's a shrewd devil, and he'd spotted in you at that one meeting something it's taken me years to recognise."

"And what did he say?"

"That you put your foot on other people's necks so charmingly that they don't know it's there."

"Oh. I thought you accused me of spoiling me, not bossing you."

"All part of the charm, and quite consistent. You're like Dad. You love me and you want to protect me, and you take it on yourself to decide my happiness for me. That's the point, Philip. In all decisions concerning my happiness, you know best. Don't you see that it's just that arrogance that has caused this trouble between us? If you'd consulted me, taken me into your confidence, those silly doubts would have been killed right away. Instead, you said, I must think this out, decide what is best for Laurian even if it hurts me. Then I'll tell her what to do. Years ago you'd decided that I should marry you and be happy with you, and, as it turned out, you were right. But you might not have been. Now, when a crisis bobs up, you again decide what is to be my fate. Whether you'll release me for Roy, or hang on to me."

"But I was only thinking of your happiness."

"And refusing to admit that I might be the best judge of that. Even if I had fallen in love with Roy again, what right had you to assume that I would want to give you up for him? Surely I should have been asked? I've fought this same attitude in Dad, and I shall fight it in you, Philip, because I won't be treated as a doll. I'm an individual, and our marriage is a partnership. If you can't see it like that, we shall come to grief, because however much you mean to me, however much our marriage means to me, I can't stifle myself, submit my mind to the domination of yours, and I don't really think at heart you'd want me to."

"No, I wouldn't. All right, my dear. I'll do my best. But I've never seen it like that, although there's something in what you say. I admit that. It's just that . . . well, I'm a bit old to change my spots now, I guess."

"I don't want you to change them, and you can't, any more than I can change mine. But don't ever shut me out while you make decisions for me, Philip. Let me be in. Let me have my say. Think how much worry and unhappiness you'd have spared yourself, as well as me, if you'd done that when Roy cropped up. Your case was all so flimsy, and so far off the mark. It never made sense, and I could have told you so long before this."

"Hold on. I'm not going to let that pass without putting up a defence. Was it so flimsy? Put yourself in my position. Suppose that you knew that Isobel and I had been deeply in love at one time and that Isobel had finally turned me down, leaving me looking like death warmed up for a long time afterwards. Suppose that you were the faithful friend in the background who persuaded me that I'd be happy if I married you. And then suppose Isobel cropped up again in like circumstances. Would you have come to different conclusions from mine?"

"No, perhaps not," said Laurian slowly, "but I shouldn't have handled it in your high-handed way."

"What would you have done?"

"When I began to feel worried, I should have said to you: 'Look here, Philip, my lad, is that old business over or is it not? Do you want to go back to that scheming, unscrupulous woman who once threw you over, or do you want to stay with me? You can't have both, so you must choose.' And then you'd have explained, and all would have been well. Quite simple, you see, if you're not convinced that you know what's best for other people," she concluded, smiling at him.

"You win. My head is bowed. Come over here and sit on my lap, and stop crowing. What would you have

done if I'd said that my heart still craved for Isobel?
No, you're not too heavy."

With her head on his shoulder, Laurian considered
this.

"I should have said 'All right. Go and take her, you
stupid creature.' And then I should have crept off to a
quiet corner and broken my heart."

"There's something to be said for the direct Vale
methods, I must say. Would you really have felt like
that?"

"Yes. To lose you now, Philip, would take every
scrap of meaning out of my life. You're part of my pattern."

"Arrogance and all?"

"Arrogance and all." she pulled his ear. "Only,
watch it."

They were quiet for a while, until Laurian said idly:

"Aren't those daffodils lovely? We don't seem to
have many bulbs coming through in the garden. At
least, I didn't see many before the snow came. Shall we
plant lots next autumn, Philip?"

"M'm. Whereabouts?"

"Under the trees and by the hedge, in big pools. And
I'd like to grow some of those special tulips Mummy
has—Parrot tulips, I believe she calls them."

"Your mother's a real gardener."

"Yes. Philip . . ."

"M'm?"

"I think I shall sell my share in the shop before the
summer. I want to have time for the garden, and you
and the home are a full-time job, anyway. I don't think
I'm the right type for divided interests. What do you
think?"

"I'm all for it, as long as you feel like that. I think
it's rather a lot for you to tackle, and, of course, all arrogant men like to be the centre of attention. I shall
just purr."

"Well, I love the sound of purring. All buttery and
happy and complacent. Besides . . ."

"Besides what?"

"Well, I suppose Dad will begin to wear an accusing

look if we don't give him some grandchildren before he's too old to instill the right principles into them. Or try to."

"You really want to?"

"Yes, darling. I wasn't sure before. Now I am. Only I rather hope we produce a batch of daughters. There have been enough men in my life. I'd like some peace."

"If we do, they'll all be independent, strong-willed Vales like you, and you still won't get peace. Perhaps life isn't meant to be too peaceful, anyway."

"Well, just here and now, it's perfect peace," said Laurian lazily.

Philip smiled and tightened his hold on her, but said nothing. At their feet, the black pup slept with his nose on the hearth and an expression of cherubic innocence on his face.

Perhaps both of them were wishing just then that time would stand still to preserve those moments of perfect happiness. But the hands of the clock moved inexorably on, the flames died down on the hearth, and the daffodils on the table flung a challenge to the fire with their promise of spring.